Who Murdered Garson Talmadge?

A Matthew Kile Mystery

by

David Bishop

TELEMACHUS PRESS

If you purchased this book without a cover you should be aware that this book is stolen property. It was reported as "unsold and destroyed" to the publisher and neither the author nor the publisher has received any payment for this "stripped book."

This book is a work of fiction. Names, characters, places and incidents have been produced by the author's imagination or have been used fictitiously. Any resemblance to any actual persons, living or dead, or to any actual events or precise locales is entirely coincidental or within the public domain.

Who Murdered Garson Talmadge: A Matthew Kile Mystery

Copyright © 2011 by David Bishop. All rights reserved, including the right to reproduce this book, or portions thereof, in any form. No part of this text may be reproduced, transmitted, downloaded, decompiled, reverse engineered, or stored in or introduced into any information storage and retrieval system, in any form or by any means, whether electronic or mechanical without the express written permission of the author. The scanning, uploading, and distribution of this book via the Internet or via any other means without the permission of the publisher is illegal and punishable by law. Please purchase only authorized electronic editions and do not participate in or encourage electronic piracy of copyrighted materials.

The publisher does not have any control over and does not assume any responsibility for author or third-party websites or their content.

Please visit David Bishop, his books and characters at http://www.davidbishopbooks.com
You may contact David Bishop at David@davidbishopbooks.com

The publisher does not have any control over and does not assume any responsibility for author or third-party websites or their content.

Cover designed by Telemachus Press, LLC

Cover art copyright © iStockPhoto # 9676660 Toe Tag;
   iStockPhoto # 11787808 Chihuahua with Pink Scarf

Published by Telemachus Press, LLC
http://www.telemachuspress.com

ISBN 978-1-937387-83-9 (eBook)
ISBN 978-1-937387-84-6 (paperback)

Version 2011.10.26

Printed in the United Stated of America
10 9 8 7 6 5 4 3 2 1

Novels by David Bishop

For current information on new releases visit:
www.davidbishopbooks.com

Titles: Release Dates

The Beholder: October, 2011

Who Murdered Garson Talmadge Octboer, 2011

The Woman: October, 2011

The Third Coincidence: February, 2012

The Blackmail Club: February, 2012

PQ's Family and other Selected Short Stories: Fall, 2012

2013-2014

The Original Alibi

Empty Promises

The Schroeder Protocol

The Red Hat Murders

Murder by Choice

To be notified when each of the above titles are available:
Send your email address to, david@davidbishopbooks.com

For more information on books and characters visit:
www.davidbishopbooks.com

Each forthcoming novel will have a new list of titles and dates.

Acknowledgments

With great appreciation I acknowledge the people who have provided invaluable assistance to the development of this particular novel: Jody Madden, Kim Mellen, John Logan, my fellow authors at Telemachus Press, so many of whom share so much, and several members of the Augusta Books and Bubbles Club. My thanks also go to Steve Jackson, Steve Himes, Claudia Jackson, Lorraine Hansen, and Terri Himes, as well as the rest of the fine staff at Telemachus Press who helped in so many ways to enhance the presentation of this novel. And, last but not least, the RGB Law Group of California who provided expertise with respect to California Pardon law and policy, licensing private investigators and the issuance of permits to carry concealed weapons. If this story contains any errors in those regards it is the failure of the author and not the experts at the RGB Law Group.

The characters who reside within this story were made smarter, tougher, sexier, or more villainous through your unselfish assistance. They join the author in saying thank you.

While this story takes place in Long Beach, California, certain dramatic license was taken to alter some things, such as the interior of the Long Beach Police Department, to fit the needs of the story.

Dedication

This novel, as are all my novels and everything I do, is dedicated to Jody Madden and my first grandchild, Brandi Bishop, whose love and encouragement continues to inspire me, my other grandchildren, Kristopher and Kaia, my sons, Todd and Dirk, all my nieces and nephews, and my various other in-laws and out-laws. Without the faith and encouragement of so many, this book would not exist.

Who Murdered Garson Talmadge

A Matthew Kile Mystery

Prologue

IT'S FUNNY THE way a kiss stays with you. How it lingers. How you can feel it long after it ends. I understand what amputees mean when they speak of mystery limbs. It's there, but it isn't. You know it isn't. But you feel it's still with you. While I was in prison, my wife divorced me; I thought she was with me, but she wasn't. She said I destroyed our marriage in a moment of rage in a search for some kind of perverted justice. I didn't think it was perverted, but I didn't blame her for the divorce.

But enough sad stuff. Yesterday I left the smells and perversions of men and, wearing the same clothes I had worn the last day of my trial, reentered the world of three-dimensional women, and meals you choose for yourself; things I used to take for granted, but don't any longer. My old suit fit looser and had a musty smell, but nothing could be bad on a con's first day of freedom. I tilted my head back and inhaled. Free air smelled different, felt different tossing my hair and puffing my shirt.

I had no excuses. I had been guilty. I knew that. The jury knew that. The city knew that. The whole damn country knew.

I had shot the guy in front of the TV cameras, emptied my gun into him. He had raped and killed a woman, then killed her three children for having walked in during his deed. The homicide team of Kile and Fidgery had found the evidence that linked the man I killed to the crime. Sergeant Matthew Kile, that was me, still is me, only now there's no *Sergeant* in front of my name, and my then partner, Detective Terrence Fidgery. We arrested the scum and he readily confessed.

The judge ruled our search illegal and all that followed bad fruit, which included the thug's confession. Cute words for giving a rapist-killer a get-out-of-jail-free card. In chambers the judge had wrung his hands while saying, "I have to let him walk." Judges talk about their rules of evidence as though they had replaced the rules about right and wrong. Justice isn't about guilt and innocence, not anymore. Over time, criminal trials had become a game for wins and losses between district attorneys and the mouthpieces for the accused. Heavy wins get defense attorneys bigger fees. For district attorneys, wins mean advancement into higher office and maybe even a political career. They should take the robes away from the judges and make them wear striped shirts like referees in other sports.

On the courthouse steps, the news hounds had surrounded the rapist-killer like he was a movie star. Fame or infamy can make you a celebrity, and America treats celebrity like virtue.

I still see the woman's husband, the father of the dead children, stepping out from the crowd, standing there looking at the man who had murdered his family, palpable fury filling his eyes. His body pulsing from the strain of controlled rage that was fraying around the edges, ready to explode. The justice system had failed him, and, because we all rely on it, failed us all. Because I had been the arresting officer, I had also failed him.

The thug spit on the father and punched him, knocking him down onto the dirty-white marble stairs; he rolled all the way to the bottom, stopping on the sidewalk. The police arrested the man we all knew to be a murderer, charging him with assault and battery.

The thug laughed. "I'll plead to assault," he boasted. "Is this a great country or what?"

At that moment, without a conscious decision to do so, I drew my service revolver and fired until my gun emptied. The lowlife went down. The sentence he deserved, delivered.

The district attorney tried me for murder-two. The same judge who had let the thug walk gave me seven years. Three months after my incarceration, the surviving husband and father, a wealthy business owner, funded a public opinion poll that showed more than eighty percent of the people felt the judge was wrong, with an excess of two-thirds thinking I did right. All I knew was the world was better off without that piece of shit, and people who would have been damaged in the future, had this guy lived, would now be safe. That was enough; it had to be.

A big reward offered by the husband/father eventually found a witness who had bought a woman's Rolex from the man I killed. The Rolex had belonged to the murdered woman. Eventually, the father convinced the governor to grant me what is technically known in California as a Certificate of Rehabilitation and Pardon. My time served, four years.

While in prison I had started writing mysteries, something I had always wanted to do, I finally had the time to do. During my second year inside, I secured a literary agent and a publisher. I guessed, they figured that stories written by a former homicide cop and convicted murderer would sell.

My literary agent had wanted to meet me at the gate, but I said no. After walking far enough to put the prison out of sight, I paid a cabbie part of the modest advance on my first novel to drive me to Long Beach, California, telling the hack not to talk to me during the drive. He probably thought that a bit odd, but that was his concern, not mine. If I had wanted to gab, I would have let my literary agent meet me. This trip was about looking out a window without bars, about being able to close my eyes without first checking to see who was nearby. In short, I wanted to quietly absorb the subtleties of freedom regained.

Chapter 1

SIX YEARS LATER:

 I was about to walk out my door to have breakfast with the tempting Clarice Talmadge and her septuagenarian husband, Garson Talmadge, without knowing Garson would be skipping breakfasts forever, not to mention lunches and dinners. The Talmadges lived on my floor, at the end of the hall in a twenty-five hundred square foot condo on the corner with a balcony overlooking the white sand shoreline of Long Beach, California. Then my phone rang. It was Clarice, but she hadn't called to ask how I liked my eggs. The cops were with her and they hadn't been invited for breakfast.

 A uniformed officer halted me at the door to the Talmadge condo. "My name's Matt Kile," I said, "I was asked to come down —"

 The saxophone voice of Detective Sergeant Terrence Fidgery interrupted, "Let 'im in."

 For seven years before my incarceration Fidge and I had worked homicides together for the Long Beach police department. Fidge was a solid detective, content with his work, a man who appeared to need nothing else. Well, perhaps a diet-and-exercise program, but Fidge was a man who would do anything to stay in shape except eat right, exercise, and drink less beer. I left the force ten years ago but stayed in touch with Fidge and his wife, Brenda, whose pot always held enough for one more plate. I often sought out Fidge for his take on the first draft of my mystery novels.

The master bedroom where Garson Talmadge slept alone was immediately inside to the right. His door loitered partially open. I could see Garson on the bed, his arm in an uncomfortable position he could no longer feel. Clarice stood in the middle of the living room, clutching her little Chihuahua to her bosom, her wet eyes pleading for help. I envied the pooch. I put my open palm straight out toward her so she would not come to me, then my finger to my lips signaling her to stay quiet.

"I'll be with you in a minute Matthew," Fidge hollered from somewhere deeper into the condo.

I waited in the foyer while the police photographer finished shooting Garson's bedroom. A liquid had been spilled or thrown against the bedroom door. I touched the wet carpet and smelled my fingers. Coffee. With cream, I thought. The photographer came out of Garson's bedroom. I couldn't place his name, but I'd seen him around. We exchanged nods as we passed in the doorway.

Sometimes you strain so hard listening for the quietest of sounds that you don't hear the loudest. The shot that had hit my neighbor just above the bridge of his nose had come so fast that before he consciously heard it, he had stopped hearing everything.

The edge of Garson's bedcovers was pulled back exposing a foot too white to be a living foot. A modest amount of dried blood soaked Garson's pillowcase, and stippling surrounded the entry wound. My elderly neighbor had taken it from up close.

I started toward the bed, heard a crunching sound and stopped. The gold carpeting between the door and the bed had been sprinkled with what looked to be cornflakes. I stood still and looked around. A man's billfold sat on the dresser in front of the mirror, the corners of a wad of cash edging out where the wallet folded over. Five boxes of cornflakes stood at attention along the wall at the end of the dresser, the flaps on the end box erect in a mock salute. At the end of the row of boxes a bottle of Seagram's Seven Crown played bookend to the cornflakes.

A hissing sound led my eyes to the sliding door entry to their ocean-facing balcony. The slider was open two inches with the air fighting its way inside like folks at the door to a popular after hour's club. The room was cold enough that I would have closed the door, but not in a crime scene. I pulled the sleeve of my sweater down over my fingertips, reached as high as my six-three frame allowed and opened the slider far enough to stick my head outside. Halfway between the door and the railing, a zigzag print from the sole of a large deck shoe smudged the dewy balcony. The sole print testified that the step had been taken toward the condo. I pushed the slider back to its original two inches. Moving carefully to avoid the cornflakes, I went into the walk-in closet. There were no shoes with that sole pattern, and no shoes of any kind under or beside the bed. Garson had always struck me as an everything-in-its-place kind of guy. His room proved it. Whatever he had worn had been hung up or dropped in a hamper. He would not have wanted to see the jagged out-of-place blood stain that defaced his pillow.

Sergeant Fidgery came through the doorway, his posture slouched, his stride short. "Hey, Matthew, I just finished your latest, *The Blackmail Club,* it's your best yet."

"Thanks, Fidge. As always, your technical tips helped. Where's your new partner?"

"What's with the new? You know George has been with me since, well, since that stupid stunt you pulled on the courthouse steps ten years ago."

"Anybody since me will always seem new. So, then, where's George?"

"Sick," Fidge said. "I'm soloing. That's why I approved your coming down here. I need you to remember how to behave in a crime scene."

"By the way, happy birthday old man. Sorry I didn't make the party last weekend. Forty-seven, right?"

"Forty-seven," Fidge said sarcastically. "We go through this every year. I'm forty-seven, you're forty-six, but only for a few months, then you'll be forty-seven like me. Brenda said to tell you she hasn't forgiven you for missing the party."

"You know I would've been there if I could. My agent scheduled a book signing way over in the San Fernando Valley without checking the date with me. She won't do that again."

"No sweat, Matthew. I'm just yanking your chain. Brenda understands."

"Thanks. Look, I stepped on the cornflakes before I saw them. They blended with the carpeting. It looks like the flakes had been walked on before I got here. You?"

"Who the hell expects cornflakes on gold carpet?" Fidge asked. "Christ, on any color carpet." Fidge put a steadying hand on my shoulder, crossed one knee with his opposite ankle and looked at his sole, then the other. Neither of us saw anything on the soles of his shoes.

"Did Clarice walk on them?" I asked.

"Says so. Says she got up, threw a load of clothes in the washer, put the coffee on, showered and slipped into what she called 'a little thing,' and then came in here to wake her old man."

"What about the uniform at the door," I asked, "did he come in, too?"

"I cursed when I stepped on the flakes," Fidge said, shaking his head. "A bit too loudly, I guess. Officer Cardiff came running. Now stop poking around, Matthew. I let the wife call you because she said she had been with you last night and that you might have a key to this place, not so's you could play detective. Tell me about her, and keep your voice down."

"What can I say? She's got her own teeth, great hair, and this and that."

"Yeah. Right off I noticed her this and that. Also the 'little thing' she put over her this and that when she got up this morning; it's hanging behind her bathroom door. You ought to take a look. Then maybe you've already seen it, with her in it." He looked at me from the corner of his eye, and then added, "I haven't heard you deny she was with you so tell me about her visit."

"Clarice came down during the night. Said she thought someone would try to kill her husband. I didn't take her seriously, but she had been right."

"What time did she get there?"

"It was dark, had been for a while. I had been zonked. I went to bed around ten. Midnight would be a good guess."

"What did she say? I want all of it and I want it exactly. Everything."

"Page one: The doorbell woke me a few minutes after midnight. I found Mrs. Talmadge leaning on my door jamb wearing a man's white button-down shirt, a strategic gap formed by the mismatching of a southern buttonhole with a northern button. Her blonde hair teased her shoulders. She had on a pair of shiny gold sandals, her toenails painted red to match the bloody mary she held, a celery stalk stood tall in the short glass."

"Knock it off, Matthew; this isn't one of your novels. You know what I want. Give."

I nodded. "Her opening line was 'something bad is gonna happen.' She brushed past me, her sandals slipping as she stepped down into my sunken living room, her shirttail failing to fully cover her backside. Oops. I forgot. You said no descriptions. I asked her what she was talking about. She said, 'somebody's going to kill Tally.' That's her pet name for her dead husband."

"Then what did she do?" Fidge asked.

"She took a big drink, chomped the end off the celery stick that had poked her in the cheek, and oozed her bottom over the arm of my leather chair, creating two small miracles. She didn't spill a drop, and her face showed no reaction when her bare bottom settled onto the cool leather."

Fidge screwed up his face.

"Okay. Okay, just the facts, Sergeant. I asked why she thought that. She said, 'Three days ago, I answered the phone. Some guy with a raspy voice asked for Gar. Only he made it sound like jar. I told him there's no jar here and hung up.'"

"Was her dead husband there?"

"No. But her live husband was." Fidge gave me the finger. I ignored his bad manners and continued. "She said her husband, sitting at the table drinking coffee, turned white when she mentioned *Gar*. To illustrate the color she held up her short white shirttail, her unblemished skin imitating melted milk chocolate. She had no tan line. I know you said to can the descriptions, but I figured you'd like that one."

"What did her husband say?"

"He told her that some former business acquaintances in Europe used to call him Gar. Then he told her to hang up when they called back."

Fidge put one hand in the air like he had been busted back to directing traffic. "When? Not if?"

"I asked her that, too. She definitely said, 'when they called back.' And, before you ask, she said there were no more such calls, at least not while she was at home. She got in Garson's face about that call again the next morning, and they again fought."

"How well did you know this guy?"

"Not all that well," I said. "I went out to dinner two or three times with the Talmadges. Garson was a bon vivant. He and I played poker with a few men in the building, maybe four times."

"Did the Talmadges go to dinner with you or did you go with them?"

"What's the difference?"

"Who invited whom?"

"I don't recall."

"Who drove? That's usually the person who extended the invitation."

"That I remember. Clarice. She gets motion sickness in a car. She found it didn't happen when she drove. Garson said it had something to do with her vision and hearing senses getting the same stimulus."

"When I was a kid," Fidge said, "my uncle always drove for the same reason. You mentioned you played poker with the deceased and a few other men in the building. The wife's about thirty-five and a real looker. The dead guy's around eighty. Was she also playing with some of the other men in the building, and I don't mean poker?"

"Yeah."

"You?"

"I expect it'll come out, so here it is. One afternoon, two days before they moved in last spring, Clarice knocked on my door. I had seen her and Garson in the building earlier, but hadn't been introduced. She said ... no, she didn't say, I assumed she and Garson were father and daughter."

"But she didn't say otherwise, right?"

"She didn't say otherwise. Before she left we did the deed, you know. Then I found out they were married. It's rumored several other fellows in the building have also taken turns. I don't know any names, but I suspect you'll find wives eager to spill their suspicions."

"Someday," Fidge said, "I need to give you my sex-without-deep-feelings-is-worthless speech. I just don't have time right now."

"Oh, too bad, I've been so looking forward to that one. But it's a load of bull. Sex for pure lust is not worthless. Not all of us are fortunate enough to have someone we love deeply in our lives every time we get a case of the galloping hornies."

"You've obviously given this a lot of thought, Matthew. But may I bring you back to why we're together this morning?"

"You brought it up." I sighed. "Go ahead."

"What do you know about Garson Talmadge's background?"

"Less than I know about his eating habits. During one of the dinners, Garson said he came from Europe, but shied from anything beyond generalities. I can tell you he spoke some words with the softer consonants common to the French. Once when the poker talk came around to Iraq, Garson pronounced 'Allah' with the back of his tongue raised to touch his soft palate as is done with Arabic."

The sun broke through the clouds to reflect off the ocean and brighten Garson's bedroom. We moved a bit to avoid the glare. Fidge walked over to look at a desk along the bedroom wall which held a computer setup and also a typewriter. "Don't see many people with a typewriter these days." Then he asked, "What else happened while she was at your place?"

"She took another bite from the celery stalk. A drip of bloody mary fell onto her skin to slalom down her abundant cleavage until blossoming into a pink splotch on her white shirt."

"Knock off the colorful bullshit, Matthew."

"You know, you're the only person since my mother who regularly calls me Matthew. Brings back memories. I like it."

"I told you to knock it off."

"Sorry. It's the novelist in me; I think that way now. Clarice said the next morning when Garson went into the bathroom, she saw a bunch of passports in an attaché case he'd left open on his bed. They all had his picture, but different names. She didn't remember any of the names, but from the way she told it he had enough to start his own phonebook."

"I understand they fought a lot?"

"According to her, yeah," I said, "at least since that call asking for Gar. She also heard him on the phone speaking some language she didn't understand. She said it wasn't French. That she didn't speak French, but had taken French in high school so she recognizes it. After the 'Gar' call, she said her husband stopped leaving their condo except to go to the workout room and spa area in the building. The only time he left the building was the prior week to keep an appointment with his attorney."

"What else?" Fidge widened his stance, taking care not to step on more of the cornflakes.

"Did I mention her fingernails were painted to match her toenails?"

Fidge flipped me off again, then asked, "What time did she leave?"

"I didn't look."

"Guess."

"I'd put it at close to four in the morning. And, yes, the skin on her fanny made a popping sound when she pulled free of the leather chair."

"She stayed nearly four hours? Just what were you two up, too?"

"We talked. All right? Her life. Well, her life some. Mostly mine, I guess."

"And you spilled your guts, right?"

"Some stuff. Yeah. The woman knows how to get a man talking."

"I'll bet she can. Her naked under a man's white shirt enhanced by mismatched buttons and buttonholes. I suppose you told her your wife got a divorce after you went to prison?"

"Yeah."

"And that she had been mad enough to file ever since you shot her father's prize hunting dog? You tell her that, too?"

"That damn dog was hunting me, Fidge, charged me in the study, saliva hanging from its teeth. For heaven's sake, you had to be there. That animal took down game with that mouth. What would you have done?"

Fidge laughed. "I'd have brought along Milk Bone when I visited the in-laws."

"Ha. Ha. Like you said, my marriage was kaput by then anyway. My arrest just gave her an easy explanation for it."

"So you sort of moved up her timetable."

"Shooting that damn dog was self-defense. Hey, you got a murder here. Shouldn't you be doing something more important than critiquing my fucked-up personal life?"

"You're right; I'm here about the murdered man, not the murdered dog. But, like we say in the crime-fighting business, you having shot the dog, then the guy outside the courthouse established your pattern of behavior. Now, you were telling me about you and Clarice and your four hours in paradise."

"I can't really tell you what we talked about. It was late. You know, you get sort of groggy, the mindless talk comes and the time goes."

Again his silent finger preceded his question. "What about the key?"

"I don't know why she said that."

"That don't answer my question, Matthew. She said you were her old man's only friend in the building. Says she figured her husband might have given you a key for emergencies or whatever. Sounds awfully convenient for when you wanted to visit with his wife."

"Okay. Here it is direct. I do not and never did have a key to the condo of Garson and Clarice Talmadge. Is that plain enough, Sergeant Fidgery?"

"Don't get hot, Matthew. You know how this works."

"I wasn't dodging your question. As for emergencies, hell, the building supervisor lets people in then. He's got keys to every unit."

"Okay. I'll check with the super."

"How do you size this up?"

The sergeant stepped closer. "The wife's a pastry on legs, but her deck is missing a few cards. She plugs her old man, and then leaves the front door dead bolted from the inside."

Fidge gestured toward a .22 revolver on the bed. "Says that there's her husband's gun, it's loaded with longs. Only one shot's been fired. I expect ballistics will show the missing long is in the old guy's brain. Says the red scarf draped over the gun handle is hers, so's that pretty little pink pillow with the ugly little black hole. Her dog sleeps on it, or used to."

"Why the pillow?" I asked. "A .22's pretty quiet. An expert would know that."

"She ain't no expert."

"Come on, Fidge." I shook my head. "Clarice isn't the kind to kill a man unless it's with loving."

"And just what kind is she, Mr. Writer?"

"The divorcing kind. She'd move on and find a new rich guy. Think of it as legal prostitution with fewer customers and better working conditions, with a topnotch severance package as a bonus."

Fidge grinned. "Maybe you should write one of them columns for the lovelorn."

I imitated his finger, using my own. "What's the story on the cornflakes?" I asked.

"Says her husband's a light sleeper. That he sprinkled the flakes on the floor so no one could sneak into his room. How's that for nutso?"

Clarice's voice shrilled from the living room. "I didn't do it, Matt. Honest to God, I didn't do it." Her chihuahua whimpered, perhaps in agreement.

I had never before heard the dog make a sound. Garson had refused to buy the condo unless his wife could keep her dog. She proved to the condo association that Asta had been trained to always stay quiet indoors and, after Garson paid a large nonrefundable deposit, Asta became the only pet in a building posted: no pets.

I looked at my old partner. "Just what points this at her?"

Fidge started with a facial expression that screamed I've already told you. He summarized: "The deadbolt. No forced entry. Nothing's missing. The neighbors have heard lots of screaming. The gun was in the house. The scarf and pillow are hers."

"That won't get you a conviction."

"That's just the part I'm telling ya. We got more and we're still in the first inning."

"What else have you that ties to her?"

"I'm not paid to report to you, Matthew. But I'll tell you this, when the wife used her scarf and her dog's pillow she moved it up to premeditated."

"Maybe Garson did himself in?" I said.

"Usually they leave a note, and suicides don't often worry about fingerprints and keeping their work quiet, not to mention the awkwardness of plugging themselves in the front of the skull."

Fidge shrugged after discrediting suicide. I agreed with him. This wasn't suicide. Still, I hadn't seen Fidge shrug that way in years, but habits become habits by lasting over time. This Fidgery shrug meant, *open and shut.*

"I'm not going to tell you again, Matthew, get outta here. The medical examiner could be here any minute."

"I'm going." I used the back of my hand to pat the sergeant on the breast pocket of his dark-blue suit coat. "She can phone her attorney after you get her downtown, right?"

"Sure."

"Who called this in?"

"Her."

"What about the coffee?" I asked.

Fidge coughed into his fist. "Says she dropped the cup when she saw the hole in her sugar daddy's noggin."

I left my ex-partner in Garson's bedroom and went to Clarice in the living room. "I'll come see you once you're permitted to have visitors."

She shifted Asta from one arm to the other while blotting her eyes with the soft pads of her straightened fingers, the way women do to avoid smudging their eye makeup.

"Please take Asta," she pleaded. "There's no one else I can ask. I got her a continental clip three days ago. She won't need another grooming for weeks. I'll be home before that."

I had once thought about getting a dog, but figured on one I could name Wolf or King. Then, after the incident with my father-in-law's mad creature, I repressed the whole idea of a dog.

"I need another minute in the victim's room," Fidge said, leaning out of the doorway of Garson's bedroom. "When I come out, I want a decision on that dog. It's you or the catcher."

"What'll I do with a little dog like that?" I asked looking at Clarice.

"She won't be any trouble." Clarice's eyes went all funny. "Please, Matt."

I had always envied the way Sam Spade could stand up to the femme fatales who tried to play him. I had given that skill to my fictional detective, but no one had given it to me.

"All right," I said, hoping I sounded less defeated than I felt. "Asta can stay with me."

"Are you sure?" she asked.

"I'm sure of almost nothing. But, yes, Asta can stay with me." I put my fingers against her lips and headed for her bedroom where I found no deck shoes with zigzag soles. I quickly looked in the bathroom, the kitchen, and the laundry room and found no zigzags there either. Fidge had likely already done this. He was a solid detective so he would have seen the shoe print on the deck and the partially open glass door in Garson's bedroom.

Back in the living room, I asked, "When did Garson start with the cornflakes?"

"Tally went all crazy after that call. He started carrying his gun around in his waistband, sleeping with it on the night stand. He kept insisting I go get six boxes of cornflakes. We fought about that. We fought about everything, about nothing. Day before yesterday, I stopped at the post office to mail a few house bills and something Tally wanted mailed to his attorney. On the way back I bought the damn cornflakes. Guess what? We still fought." She leaned closer and whispered. "He scared me real bad. I wish I hadn't —"

I grabbed her shoulders. "Save it for your attorney, you have no legal privilege over what you tell me." But she kept talking anyway.

"Damn it, I didn't shoot him. I was trying to say I wish I hadn't gotten mad at him so much those last few days." She stood clutching the dog, breathing slowly. Her eyes shut. Then she put down Asta and said, "Go with Uncle Matt."

The hair ball leaped into my arms.

"She'll sleep on the foot of your bed. You'll need to get her a new pillow. Her pink one has a ... hole in it. Take a few of her toys. She'll be fine."

Fidge again filled the bedroom doorway, "Just the mutt."

"But Asta needs her toys. She —"

"Lady. Just the mutt or we call the pound. None of this is up for negotiation."

I put my fingers under Clarice's chin, raising her head. "Get your mind off this damn dog. You're in a real mess. Do what Sergeant Fidgery tells you but don't talk about this to anyone until you get an attorney. A criminal attorney. A good one."

Fidge came out of the bedroom wearing a grin wider than his flat nose. "I hope you and Asta will live happily ever after." His eyes sort of twinkled, which is hard to imagine on the face genetics had passed down to Fidge.

"Now," he said, "for the last time, Matthew, get lost."

I lowered the dog to stop it from licking me on the mouth and walked out with Asta scrambling up my front, watching Clarice over my shoulder.

Chapter 2

LIKE YESTERDAY, TODAY started way too early. After a shower, three cups of coffee, a scan of the sports section, and four words in the crossword puzzle, I pulled my Chrysler 300 out of my building's underground parking and pointed it toward town. The veil of salty wetness that had sneaked in while the city slept still coated everything that had spent the night outdoors. I turned on the windshield wipers, hit the defroster button, and headed for the city jail. Clarice had been temporarily held at the smaller Long Beach jail inside the police department. After her arraignment, she had been moved to the larger main jail on Pacific Avenue near Twentieth Street.

Last spring, my ex-wife and I started sharing dinners, movies, and what was now her bed a few nights a week. We still cared, but she couldn't get past the anger and betrayal she felt over my having gunned down the thug outside the courthouse. After nearly a month of our running in place, I put a stop to the experiment. The ending of most relationships digs an emotional hole that refills with emptiness; ours was no exception.

Hemingway had said something like the best way to get over a woman is to get a new one. I hadn't decided whether to take Hemingway's advice or to write a novel, use her name, and have her killed–heinously. For a few weeks after I pulled the plug on our mutual effort, I considered both, a sort of double exorcism.

Then I met Clarice, who was bright and funny as well as passionate. The only problem, Clarice was married. I hadn't known that, and I hadn't bothered asking. My libido was screaming, "Any port in a storm," and Clarice was a dock slip built to hold a good sized yacht so I powered on in.

The Long Beach jail, one of California's largest, booked about eighteen thousand inmates annually. That seems like a huge number of bookings, but then Long Beach was California's sixth largest city, and America's thirty-eighth biggest with a population around half a million. To most people Long Beach doesn't seem that big, probably because it butts up to Los Angeles without an obvious border crossing.

The chairs of the Long Beach jailhouse were all occupied with people jabbering in multiple languages. I figured all of them were talking about seeing a loved one and cursing someone else for the poor choices made by the loser they had come to visit. The air felt tight from the fear which grips everyone in a jail, even those working hard at showing tough. The mothers who had brought babies were trying to keep them from crying. But the babies had it right; a jail was a place that could make anyone cry.

For now, Clarice's world was the place writers had given names like stir, the slammer, the joint, the pokie, and a thousand others. But not the big house, that name referred to prison not a jail. Whatever the name, except in the movies, escapes were rare. Once you went in, you stayed in until they let you walk out or they carried you out.

Eventually I was called through a heavy door and left to walk behind a row of uncomfortable looking chairs. Visitation was limited to fifteen minutes. I chose the first place to sit where the chairs to each side of me were not occupied by other visitors. A moment later, Clarice entered through a door like the one I had come through, only her door was on the inmate side of the glass partition. This was a big difference, huge, I could leave at will, while she would be forcibly detained. Her entrance started the clock on our fifteen minutes. She walked toward me behind a row of chairs on her side, forced a smile, not much of one, and sat down.

We were separated by a pane of glass as thick as old coke bottles. I picked up the dirty phone on my side. She picked up the dirty phone on her side. She put the flat of her other hand on the unbreakable glass, the pads of her fingers turning white from the pressure. I covered her hand with my own, the insulation of the cold glass denying the heat from her fingers.

She ignored the tide of tears spilling through her black lashes. "The prosecutor convinced the judge I was a flight risk. He denied bail. They photographed and fingerprinted me, then some dyke with a mustache long enough to curl felt me up during a strip search. After that I got shoved in the shower."

By the time Clarice finished, her voice had raised several decibels. The visiting room guard walked over and leaned down next to her. I couldn't see his face, but a good guess went something like: behave yourself or this visit's over and that gorgeous fanny of yours goes back in lockup.

She lowered her head and nodded. The guard stepped back. I gave her a minute to compose herself.

I had called ahead to get the official words. Clarice Talmadge had been charged with capital murder, also known as first degree murder with special circumstances, under California Penal Code 187 (a). The fancy title meant that if she was found guilty of having murdered her husband for financial gain, one of more than twenty different situations which constitute capital murder in California, she would face either the death penalty or life imprisonment without a possibility of parole.

Clarice jerked her hand up to swipe at a running tear. Then let her hand freefall onto her lap. Her face looked whiter than I had ever seen it, probably due to the shower and no makeup. Still, the woman was lovely. The jailhouse orange jumpsuit brought the emerald out of her bluish-green eyes. Her naturally creamy skin made me wonder why she ever bothered with makeup. Even her lips had a natural hot-pink hue, her tongue having the enviable task of keeping them moist.

She brought the phone back up to her ear.

"Asta's a strange name for a dog." I said, hoping to pull her out of her funk.

Her unpainted lips thinned and trembled. "How is my baby? Is she okay?"

"She's fine. Slept on the foot of my bed just like you said she would. We're getting along swell. I got the food and snacks you told me about. No problem. Where'd you come up with the name Asta?"

Clarice's head and shoulders swiveled to her left as a heavyset Hispanic inmate moved toward her, then quickly spun to the right to confirm the big woman had continued on by. Caught up in her jailhouse vigilance, I also watched the large woman until she sat in a chair two cubicles beyond Clarice.

"Tally bought Asta for me," Clarice said, returning from the distraction. "He named her after a dog owned by some guy named Nick Charles. I told him this Charles must be one of his friends I never met. Tally just smiled. He likes his jokes — liked his private jokes. Then he said something about my being too young to understand."

"I don't think the police are going to be looking too hard for anyone else to pin this on." It was a hard message, but one she needed to hear. She took it without reaction.

"After we met," she said, as if she had not heard my harsh message, "I researched you in the online archives. You don't know it, but I'm hot searching stuff on that Internet." She moved the phone to her other hand, the aluminum wrapped cord draping across her mouth like surreal braces. "I read all I could find about your career as a cop."

"Then you know I went to prison and why."

"I know, and I agree with the majority of the people in the poll. I'm glad you shot the bastard. He deserved it."

"I appreciate that. In any event, I doubt I would have lasted much longer as a cop."

Why?"

"The easy answer is the department thought I had too much Mike Hammer in me, while I thought the department had too much Casper Milquetoast. In my novels, I define and dole out justice the way it feels right to me. My readers must agree that justice isn't always best found in a courtroom. They keep buying my books."

"So your departmental papers show, terminated: too much Mike Hammer?"

"Well, they glossed it over as insubordination. I never have been any good at letting someone play smart when they're talking stupid, just because they're the boss."

Clarice moved in her chair, my gaze moved with her. She said, "One of the articles mentioned you're also a private detective."

"True. After my pardon they couldn't deny me a PI's license. Investigative work was my profession, but the law wouldn't allow me a permit to carry a weapon. I'm not sure why I got the private license. Maybe I thought it would add to my mystique as a crime novelist."

"Maybe because it lets you feel in some way you're still a detective." She grinned for the first time since I arrived, and then said, "The job that made you happier than being a novelist."

When they were being nice, the biddies in our building referred to Clarice as the airhead on the fourth floor, but my instincts told me Clarice was Phi Beta Kappa in street savvy.

"Me thinks the lady has brains as well as beauty."

"My mother was a lady. I think of myself as a woman. There is a difference you know?"

"No. I didn't know. As a writer, I'm naturally curious."

"When a lady sees a man who attracts her she thinks of herself as a flirt. When a woman does she thinks of herself as a prick teaser."

"I like it. May I use it?"

"Of course, but it requires you recognize one from the other."

"I'll do my best. Now, our time is limited so let's get back to your situation."

"You said the cops won't look much beyond me, so I need you to find out who killed Tally."

"Except in the pages of my books, I haven't worked a case in a lot a years. You don't want me. At best, I'm a rusty ex-detective."

"I've know a few smart men, Matt, even a couple of honest ones. But you're both. That's rare and it's just what I need."

"Don't make me out to be holy, you know my record."

"You plugging that guy shows you cared about the victim and about justice. That you're passionate about what you believe in. I need you to believe in me."

"I don't know." I kept shaking my head long after I finished saying it. "I just don't think I'm the man for this job."

"You are exactly the man for the job. You were with me. And you know I couldn't kill Tally ... You know that, don't you Matt?"

Sam Spade would easily know whether or not Clarice was working me, but I couldn't tell. In the end it mattered little, I had always had difficulty re-corking an opened curiosity.

"No promises," I said. "I'll think on it. But, as long as I'm here, I do have a question about last night."

I saw that the always perfect polish on her fingernails was now chipped when she turned the back of her hand toward me and wiggled her fingers. "Bring it on."

"When you got home from my place, did you look in on Garson?"

"No. His door was shut. He usually went to bed before me. He'd close his door when he turned off his TV. Unless he called out, I would never go in after he shut his door ... Why do you ask?"

"It would have told us whether he had been killed while you were with me or not." Her expression told me she understood.

"I expect," she said, "the autopsy will show Tally died while I was with you."

"That will show a range of time, a range that will likely cover part of the time you were with me and some time you weren't. But we don't have the autopsy yet."

She didn't say anything, just looked down and pursed her lips.

"You handling this place okay?"

She shrugged. "It's nasty and that's just the surface. Look at these outfits. How's a girl gonna look good in this ugly thing?" She tugged hard enough to billow the loose-fitting orange material over her bust, then glanced toward the door and the guard.

"You'd look good in anything," I said, meaning it, "but this is not a place for looking sensuous. Let your hair go. Don't bathe unless they insist, but cooperate when they do."

"No sweat, Matt. I hold a brown belt in karate. If any of the lesbos in this place put a hand on me, they'll wish they hadn't."

"Also, this is not a place to get in a fight. Walk and talk with confidence, not cockiness. Stay to yourself, but don't act like a victim or like you're too good for the rest of 'em."

She smiled for the second time. "Seeing we're talking outfits here, I see you wore your trench coat. That ought to help you get into your detective persona."

The trench coat may have been a little over the top into my novelist side, but I wasn't about to confess that to Clarice. "Morning fog," I said. "Wet. Now, did you get an attorney?"

"I called Henry Blackton." She stroked her fingers on the glass the way she might to tickle the open palm of my hand. "He was Tally's lawyer for all his U.S. business deals."

"You need a criminal mouthpiece, not a corporate attorney."

"That's what Blackton told me. He sent over Brad Fisher who went with me to the arraignment. I gave Fisher your name and told him you'd help. Was that okay? Do you know Fisher?"

"Only by reputation, which says he's a topnotch criminal lawyer. I've heard him called the flim-flam man. No promises, but I'll talk with him."

Chapter 3

I HAD NOT been back to the Long Beach Police Department since the day I had been taken there as the accused in what the press called, "Justice on the Courthouse Steps."

On the way over from the jail, I had tried to sort out why I was ignoring my instincts that told me not to get involved. I hadn't known Clarice was married to Garson Talmadge while we were bumping uglies. Still, under whatever conditions, when you'd done the joe buck with a man's wife you owed him something.

I had another reason for taking the case. You'll think me silly, but I'll tell you anyway. I liked Clarice. Not just because she had a full load of the B's: brains, beauty, and big boobs. I just liked her, as a person. She was plain spoken and, generally speaking, more candid than most people, male or female.

I parked around the corner from Broadway, walked back and pushed through the door. When I got close to the front desk, the uniformed officer looked up. "I'd like to see Sergeant Fidgery," I said. "My name is Matthew Kile."

"I'll let him know, Mr. Kile. Top of the stairs, take a seat. He'll meet you up there."

While waiting for Fidge, I was shocked to see how little the place had changed since I left the force. The decor was still grays and light browns with old florescent light fixtures lined up a foot or so below a white acoustical tiled ceiling that wasn't exactly white any longer. The air was the same, too, a stale mixture of sneaked cigarettes smoked in out-of-sight places, further flavored by the unforgettable aromas of farts and barf that somehow leeched in from the locker room and the drunk tank.

"Hello, Matthew," Fidge said, as soon as he stepped into sight carrying the coffee mug that he held more often than he wore pants, as least that would be my guess and I really didn't want to find out. Fidge talked with his hands and the coffee mug did its part without giving up its content. "Come on," was all he said before turning and starting down the hall without looking back.

At six-three and two-twenty I was neither short nor thin, but Fidge was six-five and over two-sixty, maybe more for he looked a bit softer around the middle, but over the years which of us don't? In the old days, the two of us had been known as the department's thundering herd. Fidge and I were more than friends. Over time our minds had culled out our case failures and hard times, while retaining the shared laughs and accomplishments. We were tight.

I strode up beside Fidge just before we turned into his office. We used to share one. Now he had a single. "I didn't get a chance to ask you at the scene, how's your wife?"

"Just fine, Brenda keeps asking when you're coming by. You know, she comes from a big family so when she cooks there's always plenty."

"Sure. New haunts. New habits. The kids?"

"Brock's good. Betty, well, if you've never had the opportunity to listen to a fifteen-year-old practicing trumpet every night, you haven't really lived." We laughed.

"Hug them all for me, will you? Tell Brenda I'll be there for Sunday breakfast. If that's not okay, let me know."

"Sunday it is, let's say nine-thirty?" I nodded. "Coffee Matthew?" he asked while approaching the pot to refill his cup.

"No thanks." Then I said, "Yeah, okay, I'll take a cup, black." Fidge smiled and brought it over to me.

We stood sipping around stern looks over the rims of our cups. I sat first. Fidge spoke first. "Have you been by lockup to see your neighbor?"

"I just left there. Grungy place."

"It's a jail, Matthew. You've been there plenty of times. But then, lately you've mostly been hanging out in bookstores and attending black-tie dinners."

"Not to mention dining on cold leftovers alone at my computer."

A picture of Brenda, Betty, and Brock, their eleven-year-old son, in his Little League uniform, sat on a gray soft-top table under the window. For me, the Fidgerys personified the modern Ozzie and Harriet Nelson family. I had told Fidge that once and he said the Adams Family seemed the better comparison.

"How're your daughters?" he asked.

"The girls are doing great. Rose, the older one is getting married soon. You'll get an invitation. Amy is trying to decide between an average-sized guy with a Bill Gates' brain and a muscle-bound athlete with one earring and several tattoos, who rides a Harley."

Fidge smiled and shook his head. "You've got to be shitting bricks. I know that craziness is ahead for me and Brenda. Betty is already eyeing the men folk in her world. Last Sunday I asked God why he let hormones grow up ahead of brains. How do we get these youngsters to understand the only really important thing about high school is graduating? That the rest that they think is so important won't mean squat in the big picture of their lives?"

"One of life's easy questions, with no easy answer, at least I don't have one for you."

"And Helen?"

"Ah, my ex. No easy answer there either. Last year she came close to remarrying, but didn't. The girls are her life right now, along with keeping track of my doings. If I didn't know better, I'd swear the woman was listening to my life on the upstairs extension."

"Sounds like she still cares."

"If she did, she would have stood with me during my trial."

"Your attorney should have gotten her there."

"I told him to leave her alone, that coming or not was her decision."

"She was hurt. Confused. Angry. For that matter, so was I, but I also understood why you sent that guy to hell; your ex didn't. But she ended up writing while you were inside, didn't she?"

"For the first couple years, she did. Then she stopped. I couldn't figure her then. I still can't. Hey, I feel silly sitting in your office while you stand."

Fidge didn't move. After taking another drink of his coffee, he said, "You know I can't discuss this case with you."

"I understand, Fidge. I just came by so we could sit and look at each other, but you aren't even sitting. Listen, I don't believe Clarice did it. I got nothing except instinct working here, but, like I said, unless he died of an overdose of bed banging, killing's not her style."

"Oh, you got firsthand knowledge about that, Matthew?" Fidge unhooked his top button to free his moose-sized neck from his deer-sized collar.

"You know what, Sergeant Fidgery, You're a dirty old man." We exchanged more grins. "I just can't see her bumping off her old man," I said, feeling myself slipping deeper into the brand of cop and street vernacular spoken in my modern-noir novels. "If she plugged 'im, it woulda been in the heat of passion or anger, and she would've been looking him straight in the eyes. She'd have no interest in pillows to muffle the shot. She'd wanna hear it. She'd wanna smell the cordite. Even then, I can't see her doing it."

Sergeant Fidgery wedged his thumbnail between his two front teeth. He must have gotten whatever he was after because his eyes crossed when he looked just before licking his nail.

"People aren't as predictable as the characters in your novels, Matthew. You told me once that characters have to act consistent with their personalities."

"Their true personalities," I retorted, "which might be very different from the ones they show the world."

Fidge ignored my cleanup of his comment and continued. "That's swell in those books of yours, but not necessarily in real life. Real folks often act outside the mainstream of their lives. They go off the deep end and kill or rob and run. Hell, you know that. You were a damn good cop long before you started writing. Bottom line: This guy Talmadge was a respected, retired businessman. Somebody's gotta pay and the bill's got his wife's name on it."

"Fidge, shady businessmen are like politicians and madams, they get respectable only after they get dead."

Fidge held up his mug in a silent offer of more coffee. I shook him off and waited while my former partner refilled his cup from a pot sitting on a hot plate atop another gunmetal-gray table butted into the corner. He carried his cup to my side of his desk, slid his backside over its top edge, leaned toward me, and spoke low. "It'd be like old times to discuss this case with you, but damn it, you know I can't, really can't."

He circled back around his desk and before finally sitting down, placed his cup randomly among the brown rings commemorating the countless cups that had sat near him before this one.

"No problem, Fidge, we won't talk about it. I'm just saying she didn't do it. Women like her see their bodies as tools and marriage as an investment. For them, no man is worth prison. They don't ever see themselves as jilted or betrayed. They just move on, seduce a new honey, and figure the next one'll be a better deal."

My ex-partner smirked like he'd known a few, or maybe like he had fantasized knowing just one.

"Fidge, that scene just didn't add up. You got her using a pillow for quiet. You got her using a scarf to avoid prints, and showering after the shooting. You have her planning it down to tossing a cup of coffee against the bedroom door to illustrate her shock at finding her husband dead. Then you see her as leaving the deadbolt latched till you arrive and telling you it had been locked all night. That's half smart, half super stupid. She would've unlatched the dead bolt before you arrived, and said, 'Gee, that's odd, Sergeant Fidgery, it's usually locked. My husband must've let someone in after I went to bed.' Come on, Fidge. I admit you got a nice bundle of circumstantial, but you've also got contradictions galore. I doubt they'll dance together in front of the grand jury."

Fidgery hooded his eyes and again gave me his case-closed shrug.

A year or so before I shot my way out of the department, we had a case where an older husband was killed. His wife, a real looker, a graduate of Plastic Surgery U., had been a suspect, but Fidge refused to believe anyone that angelic could kill. Well, she had done it and Fidge endured being razzed until the trial ended and she was found guilty. After that he figured every good-looking female suspect was Lynette Squeaky Fromme.

I had gone in expecting to get his views on the zigzag footprint and the open glass slider, but Fidge had decided Clarice had done it so I let it lie. Instead, I said, "You know one of the side effects of all that coffee you drink is irritability."

He gave me the finger again. I said, "What's this thing with your finger? You trying to recapture your adolescence?"

"Saves time while capturing the sentiment."

"Maybe you should try decaffeinated coffee or no-caffeine soda?"

We went mum on the Talmadge case after that and relived a few wing dings from the old days.

I walked out of Fidge's office, and got to the stairwell with my hand on the rail to start down to the ground floor when I heard my name. "Matthew." I turned to see Fidge standing in the hall just outside his office. "Come back here!" While he waited, he used his thumbs to pull up on the front of his trousers.

I went back in while his trousers went back down to their original position.

"Your nympho neighbor needs a good attorney. We got lots more. A damn good attorney, Matthew. Now get the hell out of here. I got work to do."

Chapter 4

THE GOSSIP GAGGLE in my condo development had long ago decided that Clarice had boffed the entire building's population of husbands. I knew two things about that: it was at least partially true, and Clarice enjoyed the rumors. She loved tantalizing the old prunes. I didn't know whether they were envious of the body Clarice had, that they didn't, or the sex Clarice was getting, that they weren't, probably both. One thing was certain. They would all do the witness dance for the D.A.

I had lied to Fidge. It hadn't been a big lie, only a tactical one. Clarice and I had spent more time together than I had confessed, but I hadn't lied for the reason you're thinking. We had no ongoing affair. Not that I didn't want to, but Clarice was married. Yeah, I know, you can call me provincial and you'd likely be right, but I prefer principled.

Garson Talmadge was a cold man who, from what I determined, cared deeply only about money. He had neither strong passion nor compassion for anything or anybody standing between him and his next profit. For him, people were tools.

So you don't get the wrong idea, let me confess I also like money, more than most people I'd guess, but far less than Garson Talmadge. Of course, I admit that money is something about which one can be more principled after they have an adequate supply.

Clarice, on the other hand, was all about passion and compassion, well at least passion. Not that she didn't like money, she did. That was why she married Garson. She had made her deal with him and from what I'd seen, she was holding up her end. On some level, she cared for him. She cooked for him. And she gave him all the sex he could handle. Because her desires far exceeded his, they had also agreed that she could venture into the beds of other men. Garson asked only that she not flaunt doing so. That part was hard for if Clarice was breathing, Clarice was flaunting. No doubt, their arrangement was certainly a nonstandard plank in marital vows, but in their case it could also be seen as pragmatic. Garson wanted a trophy wife, and Clarice wanted to be assured she would be taken care of after his demise. This was a marriage of convenience. Still it appeared to me to be going smoothly until someone punched Garson's ticket.

Let me get back to my coming clean about my clandestine relationship with Clarice. First, I should admit, having visited her warm places that one time, I was eager for a return visit. People go where they are invited and return to where they were made to feel welcome, and Clarice had made me feel very welcome. I enjoyed my time with her. She was more intelligent than the building biddies thought, much more so, and she had a quick wit. She considered my standard about no married women to be based on some boyhood notion of honor. I didn't agree. We let that be and focused on being friends, sharing time now and again after Garson went to bed. She continued trying to entice me, but I held to my principle while enjoying her enticements, all the while wishing I'd change my mind. But, principles don't really exist if one abandons them when the going gets tough, or, in this instance, the temptations get great.

I know what you're thinking, this guy shot somebody he figured deserved to die, but he won't have sex with a willing married woman who held a hall pass from her husband. What can I tell you? Life is rarely neat, and often confusing.

Just as I put my hand on the banister to pivot off the bottom stair onto the first floor, I heard someone holler, "Hey, Mr. Kile."

This time the voice didn't belong to Fidge, but to the desk sergeant. "Mr. Kile," he repeated, lifting the hinged end of the front counter and coming toward me. "Chief of Detectives, Richard Dickson, has instructed me to escort you to his office."

Not wanting to look chicken, I followed the sergeant into the elevator. "Chief Dickson's office is on the third floor," the sergeant said. The door closed in the middle, making that hollow sadistic sound that elevators make just before the floor turns to mush.

Don't misunderstand, I'm not a wimp. I just don't like elevators so I avoid them whenever it's practical. I can handle airplanes, and heights are manageable when I walk up. But every time I get in an elevator I feel like Jimmy Stewart in the Hitchcock movie *Vertigo*. It's a bullshit condition, and I know it has no foundation in fact. Still, I've fought that sense of panic all my life, with off-and-on progress.

The sergeant pushed the button for three. "I'm a big fan, Mr. Kile. I really enjoy your books."

"Thank you, Sergeant. Call me Matt."

My mouth went dry as the elevator groaned and moaned. That sensation grew into nausea when the box-on-a-cable staggered passing the second floor. Actually, this time was not so bad. Most often the clammy panic came as soon as the doors closed. A bright green number three appeared above the door just as a dollop of sweat gathered on my forehead. The elevator navigated its up-and-down bounce, stopped, and, to my relief, proved that its doors, once closed, would again open.

We walked to the end of the hall where the desk sergeant knocked on the wood panel framing the fogged glass that read: Captain Richard Dickson, Chief of Detectives.

Behind his back, Chief of Detectives Richard Dickson's name was "Two Dicks." Politics and the Peter Principle had danced in the street the day Dickson made CD.

A long quiet minute passed before a guttural voice leached through the door. "Come in."

While the sergeant reached for the door, I swiped at the sweat run gathering speed as it worked through my sideburn. We walked inside.

The Long Beach Chief of Detectives had a wooden desk, an upgrade from the soft gray-top in Fidge's office. The room had one window. The blinds were drawn. The walls were crowded with pictures; the most prominently placed being one showing the ambitious man smiling and shaking hands with the chief of police. Another showed Dickson shaking hands with the mayor. In the next, Dickson stood before the U.S. flag, shaking hands with our local congressman. In it, Dickson was illustrating that he had political connections, while giving the congressman the opportunity to display a tough-on-crime image. On the side wall were a dozen or so photos of smiling Dickson standing with a gaggle of civic, religious and business leaders. There was also a picture at some black tie gala in which I thought Clarice was standing a few feet behind Dickson, but the woman was far enough in the backdrop, that I couldn't be certain it was she.

The last picture I glanced at had him holding a shiny shovel with a small dollop of dirt at a groundbreaking somewhere. Well, you get the idea. The walls were further adorned with plaques and awards — probably for coddling criminals. One thing conspicuously missing was family pictures. Even single men had families, but there were no pictures of Dickson's parents or siblings, if he had any. Siblings, I mean. He had to have parents, or so I assumed.

I had to give credit where credit was due. The man was tall and fit and gussied up in a black pinstriped double-breasted suit with a matching blue tie and pocket hanky. He looked more politician than cop. While a detective, the man had solved crimes at an alarming rate, and quickly advanced through the ranks to become the city's first ever unmarried chief of detectives. He was also known as a lady's man, with his picture often featured on the society page escorting one or another of Long Beach's wealthy young widows. No way could Dickson be confused with the overweight, rumpled detectives chewing on soggy cigar butts with whom the fictional Phillip Marlowe had regularly matched wits.

"That's all, Sergeant," Dickson said, looking up after having made us wait long enough to establish his importance. "Kile, stay."

His command for me to stay sounded like the commands I had been trying with Asta, and I didn't obey any better than Clarice's chihuahua.

"Listen, Dickson, if you got something to say, be polite or you can go to hell." After I said it, I heard the office door latch shut. I hadn't planned for that, but, given how the rank and file felt about Dickson, the desk sergeant hearing it was more good than bad.

Perhaps that had been Asta's meaning when she turned and walked out of the room after I had ordered the little thing to stay.

"Thank you, Mr. Kile," Dickson snarled, before patting his neatly trimmed mustache as if it were a loose glue-on. "That segues into why I wanted to see you. Sit."

No real cop said words like "segue," so I now had one more reason to dislike the jerk.

"I hear just fine standing." I shifted into a sarcastic parade rest stance, my hands together against the small of my back. I also decided that tonight I'd try a different tone with Asta. I had read somewhere that a relationship can be built on mutual understanding so maybe Dickson and I had a future. But for now and as far ahead as I cared to look, I didn't like Two Dicks, never had, and I knew it cut both ways.

Color rose to Dickson's cheeks and his eyebrows arched above his shit-brown eyes. "Citizen Kile, you've been washed up around here since you stopped catching murderers and became one. Except for that play-school badge you carry, you're no longer a detective. You're a writer and not a very good one at that. You're a civilian." His pointing finger hovered between us. "So stop thinking you can just waltz in here whenever you have a notion to talk to Sergeant Fidgery or any of my detectives."

"Okay. I heard your message. Now hear mine." I moved out of the imaginary line from Two Dick's finger. "I used too much muscle for you and the other do-gooders so caught up in protecting the rights of the crud that you've forgotten about protecting the honest folks."

"Get lost, citizen." The pointy finger again.

"Not yet. Got one more thing to say." I leaned my thighs against his desk.

"Spill it and then blow."

"And then blow? You been watching old gangster movies, Two Dicks? Okay, here it is in noir gangster speak, lemme give it ta ya straight, see, 'cause this ain't just about you and me, see. I came to talk with Sergeant Fidgery for good reason. I knew last night's victim, Garson Talmadge, also the dame you're trying to pin it on, his wife, Clarice Talmadge. And here's a flash. She didn't do it. They're my neighbors, see. It's Sergeant Fidgery's job to talk to folks like me. I came down of my own volition to answer his questions about the two of 'em. So don't get your nose out of joint toward Fidge — Sergeant Fidgery."

Dickson glared at me. His moment of silence gave me an opening and I took it. Often it is good strategy to say something you aren't sure of as if you are. If you're right, people will often not correct you. It works better than just asking a question to which yes or no is an equally correct answer. I framed the first part of what I said next in that spirit. "You know the accused, Clarice Talmadge. Certainly you agree she would not commit murder."

"I've never met the woman." Dickson had corrected my statement which strongly suggested he didn't know Clarice. However, it could also mean he had something to hide and, as an accomplished interrogator, understood why I had phrased my question as a statement and so he had disagreed. I still figured he knew her. After all, he had a pecker and Clarice collected 'em.

I took the picture down from his wall and dropped it on his desk. "There you are." I pointed. "There she is." I pointed again.

He picked up the picture. "If that's the woman Sergeant Fidgery booked in, she wasn't with me. She's in the background like a lot of other people who were there that I didn't know."

"I understand that now you wouldn't want to know her. Not with her being arrested for murdering her husband. It wouldn't exactly be tidy for an ambitious chief of detectives."

"Believe what you will, writer, I could care less."

"I will, Two Dicks."

"All right, you've had your say. Get lost. If I see you around this department again, I'll have you arrested."

We spend a full minute exchanging screw-you looks. Then I walked out.

Chapter 5

THE LOBBY IN Brad Fisher's office included a photograph of four men in golf attire. The plaid pants and wide white belts told me this particular golf outing had occurred quite some years before. I recognized one of the four men, Dick Fisher. The receptionist said Dick was Brad's brother. I had met Dick on the golf course a few years ago, when I was still playing golf. I'm going to play again, you understand. I haven't quit. I've just retreated. When I find the right set of clubs for my kind of swing, I'll be back out there. Someday I plan to shoot my age. It's one of those goals a man sets for himself to prevent fully abandoning the little boy that secretly lives inside. And, one day, I will shoot my age, if I live long enough.

Dick Fisher is an OB-GYN; which tells me Dick was smarter than his brother, Brad, who, as a criminal lawyer, spends his days dealing with assholes.

Brad Fisher came out to greet me. I liked that. It was less high hat than having me ushered in to first see him sitting behind some whale-sized, hand-rubbed desk. We got coffee, which Brad schlepped himself, another gesture that labeled him a down-to-earth guy. We got right to it.

After a lot of discussion and some argument, Fisher convinced me to become his investigator, part of his defense team. Truth was, I had already made up my mind to look into Garson's death. Working for the defense would legitimize my digging and grease my access to some information. The nasty part, Fidge and I would be on opposite sides. But I had realized that from the start.

Then again, maybe Clarice had been right, maybe I had gotten a PI license because I still liked to think of myself as a detective. That could also explain why I had taken on the investigation. In any event, I wasn't altogether comfortable with my refresher course coming in a matter that could jeopardize the woman's freedom, maybe even her life. It would also be disingenuous if I did not admit I lusted to see a grateful Clarice in something more fetching than jailhouse orange. Clarice was now a widow which meant, under my code, she was back in play.

Garson Talmadge's children, born Sappho and Charaxus, but known as Susan and Charles, had given statements to the cops that their stepmother, Clarice, must have killed their father. The son, Charles, told Sergeant Fidgery his father had called the night of his death, around two in the morning and that his father had said he was going to change his will to leave nothing to his wife. This meant Clarice would only get the one million she was promised in their prenuptial. The daughter, Susan, said Charles had called her right afterwards to share the news from Daddy, or Papa as they called Garson.

Like most attorneys, the litigators anyway, Fisher had his office within an easy walk of the courthouse. Also nearby were several restaurants and a couple of Long Beach's upscale watering holes, where more pleas were bargained and settlements reached than in all their paneled conference rooms.

Garson's corporate attorney, Blackton, had confirmed to Brad Fisher that Garson had called to set an appointment to change his will. At the time, Blackton had been on the way to the courthouse, so they had not talked long.

"They were going to meet next week," Fisher went on to say. "Wishful thinking would say that Talmadge had decided to drop his kids from his will. They got wind of it, killed him and framed their stepmother. The prosecution will argue Garson wanted to cut out Clarice, and the D.A. has the son's testimony supporting that claim. On top of that he has Garson's attorney lined up to confirm that Garson had planned to change his will. I can get Susan's testimony stricken. It's hearsay because she heard it from her brother, not directly from her father. I should have a copy of Garson Talmadge's will tomorrow. The big problem is the prosecution's contention is the more credible: that an elderly man would be more likely to drop his nubile wife from his will than to cut off his children. This point will score big for the prosecution. And it keeps getting better for the D.A.'s office," Fisher added. "Clarice was the only person in the locked condo with her dead husband. The scarf and pillow used in the shooting were hers, the gun her husband's. A jury would figure any other shooter would have brought his own tools. It's all circumstantial, but short of an eye witness, the D.A. has an effective game plan."

"Hell, Brad," I said, trying to put something on the other side of the scales of justice. "Garson's kids have lots of reasons to lie. If Clarice is found guilty, the two kids will likely split the millions she would have gotten under the executed will."

"Five million is the number that fits in your comment. The unchanged will, the only will at the time of his death, gives her five million with about ten more to be split between Susan and Charlie."

"So," I said, quickly doing the math, "the kids each get an extra 2.5 mil. Lots of murders have been done for less."

"Not quite. The prenuptial guarantees her one million, so each of the kids would net an extra two mil. But, Matt, may I call you Matt?" I nodded. "We're facing their testimony about the phone calls and, for now, we have to assume the D.A. will produce phone records confirming Garson called his son who then called his sister. He'll have Blackton for corroboration to the extent that Talmadge did plan to revise. Now, for the whipped cream and cherry: The jury, being mothers and fathers themselves, will want to accept any argument other than children kill their fathers for money. As for the greed of the two children, if Garson had planned to drop Clarice from his will, the kids could've done nothing and ended up splitting the other five mil, well, four, net of the prenup. So they don't appear to have even a financial reason for killing their father."

"Other than the *more and sooner rule*," I offered in weak counter. "More money is better than less and getting it sooner is better than getting it later. They'd get more money and receive it sooner with Daddy dead and their pigeon convicted."

"I need you to primarily focus on those two kids," Fisher said. "Find me some dirt to sprinkle on 'em, anything that might give them a motive to kill their father. If we can discredit them, even a little, I can take a chunk out of the D.A.'s foundation. I also want you to find out where the kids were the night Garson was killed."

"Maybe Garson killed himself to make it look like Clarice did it?" I asked without much enthusiasm.

"At this point, anything's possible," Brad said with his reply matching my comment for lack of enthusiasm. "But we have no reason to believe he hated his wife enough to punch his own ticket to frame her. While you're working the kids' angle, I'll check into his health and state of mind, but for now we've got no clothesline on which to hang suicide."

"What have you learned about Garson's business affairs?" I asked. "Around the building, he always changed the subject when talk swung toward how he'd made his dough."

Brad stood up and moved out from behind his desk. After looking down, he pinched his left trouser pleat, raised the pant leg and then released it. The cuff had been hung up on the lace of his wingtip. Then, with his slacks shipshape, he continued.

"There's no reason for secrecy now that Talmadge is dead. Blackton told me old man Talmadge was a dealer in weapons who primarily sold to Saddam Hussein, brokering for some unnamed French munitions manufacturers. Blackton doesn't know specifics because he only represented Talmadge in his U.S. business and personal dealings. Blackton did, however, allege that Talmadge told him he had stopped selling weapons after he got U.S. citizenship."

"We got ourselves a small contradiction," I said. "The kids told Sergeant Fidgery that their father stopped dealing weapons fifteen years ago, five years before the three of them came to the States. Now Blackton told you that Talmadge said he stopped after he got his citizenship which was about ten years ago."

"I know Blackton," Fisher said, "he's as big a dove on defense as there is, so it figures Blackton wouldn't have anything good to say about anyone in that business. I think he's trying to help me as much as he can. That started when he referred Clarice to me. To be clear, though, Blackton didn't say Talmadge was still running guns. That's just me covering the possibilities. You know something, that old man must have had a real crust on him. I mean, selling death. Then again, I suppose everyone has some good points."

"I suppose," I said with a shrug. "But some folks keep them well hidden."

Brad Fisher and I went on to discuss the more likely Plan B: French arms manufacturers and politicians as well as Middle East conduits were worried. Their concern: weapons found in Iraq would be traced back to Talmadge who, to protect his American citizenship, might be squeezed into talking. That seemed more likely than kids killing their papa, but any good investigator follows up more than one lead. Most don't pan out, a few do. It's a numbers game.

Chapter 6

GARSON'S DAUGHTER LIVED on the second floor of an older, two-story stucco-and-wood building about a block from what the locals called Cherry Beach. Cherry was a little sandy inlet near Belmont Shore, a tired, but not an unattractive neighborhood populated with beach lovers who come in all ages and sizes. For decades, foxy chicks have loitered on the Cherry to attract stares before feigning indignation at being gawked. Nothing about that had changed much over the decades except for the shrinkage of women's bathing suits — one of the very few ways the modern world had improved the good-old days.

The records in Brad Fisher's office showed Susan Talmadge to be thirty-eight years old, the same age as her stepmother, Clarice. No, I never asked Clarice her age. Once a man got to know the modern woman he could ask if she was wearing a bra, even panties, but it would always remain tacky to ask her age. Clarice had once told me she was exactly half her husband's age, and I had attended Garson's seventy-sixth birthday the month before.

I got to Susan Talmadge's place around noon, a fourplex, two on the ground with two above. I walked up wooden stairs and after two rings, separated by reasonable patience, I rang once more, but my heart wasn't in the third attempt. No answer was the risk of coming without being expected, but I didn't like people I planned to interrogate to have prior notice of my arrival.

On the way down the steps, my eyes stopped on one of the well-tanned feminine refugees from Cherry Beach crossing at the nearby intersection. She was a full grown woman, not one of the older teens or young twenties that were common in the area. She wore a yellow bikini, which except for not having the polka dots, could have been the itsy, bitsy, teeny, weenie, yellow-polka dot bikini made famous in a 60's song.

Through a well-executed plan I got to the bottom of the stairs just as she arrived at that point on the sidewalk. I admit the plan was a bit adolescent, but most men from their teens to their final days remain adolescent about shapely women with abundant cleavage, so I felt a certain duty to maintain my good standing in the men-of-the-world club.

"May I help you?" Her hand rested on the railing, her little finger touching the side of my hand.

With the way she filled that bikini, she could definitely have helped me, but instead of going with that thought, I held firm to my manners. "Excuse me?" I asked.

"You just came down from my front door. And you're blocking me from going up. So, how can I help you?"

"Are you Sappho Talmadge?"

"Sappho is the name on my birth certificate. But please call me, Susan. Not Sue. I hate that."

I introduced myself. We shook hands. Her come-on smile plus her curves totaled up to wow! As for me, if my smile could walk it would have stumbled.

She turned sideways and came onto the stairs, our noses and more nearly bumping as she edged past me. I had come to surprise her, to catch her off guard. Instead, she had surprised me.

I followed her yellow and tan parts up the stairs while trying to maintain my composure, and remember what I had come to find out.

Once inside, I said, "Let's start fresh. My name's Kile. Matt Kile."

"You're not exactly a small man are you?"

"I tried to be. It just didn't work out."

She didn't offer me a tour, but a quick look around revealed she had an obvious flair for decorating. Excellent contemporary furniture nicely accessorized with pillows and paintings, a modern kitchen off the living/dining room, and a patio with an unobstructed view of the Pacific, complete with a space heater, surf and gull sounds. And a swing, not at all like the rope and tire hanging from a tree that my brother and I shared as kids. This was a small swing suspended by white nylon rope, with a padded seat adorned by a pleasantly sized impression that told me Susan sat there often.

She brought out a pitcher of iced tea, poured two glasses, and sat on the lower half of her yellow two-piece swim suit. The upper yellow piece — I didn't know the right name for that kind of top, oysters on the half shell came to mind — but I had never seen an oyster of that size jiggle like that. Actually I had never seen an oyster of that size, jiggling or stationary; but I digress. The half shell nearly disappeared when she cinched her crossed arms under her breasts. Her body reminded me of her stepmother, Clarice, their playful sensualities also being very similar. I'm proud to say I also remembered the first question I came to ask.

I took a small sip of tea and steadied myself the way men always have in such circumstance, I glanced at her cleavage. It's my theory that women who show cleavage want men to look, just not to leer. Men can allow their thoughts to linger, just not the looks. I didn't disappoint her or myself; the look didn't linger, but my thoughts did. Then I swam deeper into the water that had washed me onto her shore. "Tell me about your relationship with your stepmother."

"She's got a great little pooch. That Asta is a real sweetie pie. Where's the dog now?"

"Asta is with me."

"With you?"

"Yeah. I've never had a dog. Always figured that one day I'd get a man's dog, but, it's temporary, just until Clarice gets out."

"Gets out! That bitch is a murderer, or is it a murderess? She married Papa for his money. When Papa wised up to that fact and decided to drop her out of his will, she killed him."

"She could have filed for a divorce," I countered. "California is a community property state. That presumes a 50-50 split of assets."

"Presumes?" She huffed, and then crossed her legs, leaving her top foot bobbing up and down the way I'd seen lots of women foot bob. And come to think of it, I've never seen a man foot bob. "The signed prenuptial," she said, "establishes that all Papa's assets were his sole and separate property. In it, she agreed not to make any claim challenging that point. In return, Papa agreed that she would get a minimum of one million as long as she stayed with him until he died or ended the marriage. The prenuptial also acknowledged he could use his will to leave her more if he chose to, but that he could change his will anytime at his sole discretion. His executed will stipulates Clarice will get a full third along with Charlie and me. If Papa took her out, she would be back to the one mil in the prenup. That's your motive: about four million dollars."

"You sound like a lawyer." I said, while watching her reverse the top gam in her crossed pair. The new top foot was not a bobber.

"And you strike me as a man pretty much at ease with himself."

"I know who I am, what I believe in. But you haven't answered me. I asked if you were a lawyer."

"No, you didn't. You said I sounded like a lawyer. That's a statement, not a question."

"That sounded like a lawyer, too. Are you an attorney?"

"I graduated from law school more than a year ago; I started later in life. Since then I've not taken a job. Papa provides my brother and me with an annual stipend. With that and some part time work, I get by. I'll likely take serious employment some day. Not sure if it'll be the law. Just haven't had to decide, I guess."

Actually I already knew that Susan had gone to law school. Clarice told me that Susan had attended the U.C.L.A. School of Law, but Clarice wasn't certain if Susan had graduated. I checked. She had, with honors.

Susan uncrossed her legs, slid out of her sandals, and pulled her feet up onto the couch sideways, turning herself toward me. I waited patiently, watching the entire maneuver and could not have imagined it being done with more ... how should I describe it, style?

"What kind of part time work?"

"I work at a few gentlemen's clubs in the area. Strictly fill in. ... Ah, yes. The look. Your middle-class judgment."

"No. No. That's your business."

"I saw your expression. You pulled it back, but it had already come. Just for your information, I don't hook. I give it away to whomever I choose. At the clubs, I do some pole, frankly pole is really healthy work. I also do laps, mostly younger men wanting a new experience, and you middle-aged guys."

"Ouch. That should even us up after my look, as you called it."

"Do you want to change the subject?"

"I wish I had a few minutes ago." We shared one of those brief, polite laughs. "Tell me about your mother."

"I'm not clear on how that is relevant," she said in mild protest, "but I don't mind. Our mother was Iraqi. Charlie and I are twins."

"Did your dad live in Iraq when you two were born?"

"No. Papa made business trips to Baghdad. I don't know all that much about it. He went there a few times a year. That's how he met our mother. I hate to admit it, but I don't even know her name. Papa told me once when we were young, but I just don't remember."

"Were you raised in Baghdad?"

"No. When we were babies, Papa brought us to France where we grew up. He had a wife in Paris and the three of us, Papa, Charlie and I lived with her, and Papa continued his business trips to the Middle East. Ten years ago Papa divorced his French wife, and we moved to the U.S. and became citizens."

"Where did your father meet Clarice?"

"Here. America," she said, then narrowed it still further, "Long Beach. Rumor is she worked as an escort, but in fairness, we don't know that for certain. Ask her. She's your client. Although, I suspect, you've been formally retained by her attorney, this Fisher guy."

"You know you two, Clarice and you, look a bit alike, aside from your slightly darker complexion."

"It's okay to say what you mean: our bodies are very similar. We wear the same size clothes. She's a C-cup, I'm a D, other than that we're the same. We have never shared clothing, however. May I ask you something, Mr. Kile?"

"Sure, but drop the Mr. Kile."

"Matthew?"

"I prefer Matt." *Although the way you say 'Matthew' sounds a lot hotter than when Fidge says it.*

"All right, Matt. Why are you helping that bitch? She murdered Papa."

"She's only accused, not convicted. You know that, being a law school grad."

"Technically speaking that's true, but there's no doubt. I've explained her motive. So, why are you helping her?" Susan again crossed her arms below what she had described as D cups. I let my look linger, breaking the rule. She reached over, put her fingers under my chin and raised my stare back to her eyes.

"She was with me that night," I said, "early into the next morning. I don't believe she did it."

"I see." She raised her eyebrows this time. "You two have a thing?"

"Clarice had come down to talk with me, scared someone might kill your father. She was frightened. I tried to console her." I went on to tell Susan about the call for Gar — Jar — it would all come out anyway.

"She came down after Papa had gone to bed for the night," Susan said, continuing her accusatory tone. "I can imagine how you consoled her, how she would want you to console her."

"Nothing happened that night."

"But you two have shared the sheets. Clarice loves to get it on. She told me so one night when we were both a bit soused. Papa knew she did, and he understood she had needs he could no longer fulfill. Still, she was always there for him when he could. I give her that much."

"When they first moved in, I thought your father was her father."

"Hey. It would have been out of character for her not to seduce you. Matt, you are too much a hunk for her to pass up."

Susan got up, stepped around the coffee table and faced me teasingly while leaning forward to refill our tea glasses.

I crossed my legs, the effect being nothing like when she had crossed hers. I added a throat clearing. She sat back down, trumping both my leg crossing and throat clearing.

"Okay," I said, "we've established where I was the night your father was killed. Where were you?"

"I danced at the club until it closed at two. Right after that my brother called. A few of the other girls and I got out of there about two-thirty and went to an all-night diner for some early breakfast. Working on a pole can build up an appetite."

"I imagine it would for her; for me I'd work up the appetite watching her work the pole. Where was your brother that night?"

"All I know is he was home when he called me. He must have been out on his deck because I could hear his wind chimes. Let's be a little less serious for a minute here. Can I get you something stronger than ice tea? I've got most anything you'd want."

"Irish whiskey?"

"No. I'm sorry. I'm going to get some wine. Join me?"

"Sure. That'd be nice."

"Its white wine. Okay?"

I nodded, although I had never really known if white wine was for drinkers or people who wished to appear to be sophisticated drinkers.

She came back a moment later carrying two stemmed wine glasses. The wine was obviously cold for the glasses were dressed in condensation. "Are you Irish?" she asked.

"With a name like Matthew Kile, what's to doubt? But if you want proof, I'll let you pet my leprechaun."

"I've never heard it called that before. I guess it's small." She frowned. "All leprechauns are small, or so I'm told."

"Not too many Irishmen go around showing each other their leprechauns, so I don't really know how mine might compare with other leprechauns."

"Will it stand at attention and take orders?"

"Willie sometimes has a mind of his own, but Willie lives to serve, my good woman."

"Willie, huh, I guess yours must be special to have a name."

"I'm going to change the subject now, if that's all right?"

"Sure. We can come back to Willie at any time. As you said, it lives to serve; I assume that includes damsels in distress."

"The story is that your dad was a broker of illegal weapons. True?"

"He did some of that, years ago. He quit before we left France. Not that quitting made his doing it okay, but it does make it old news."

She stood again and went to the glass sliding door. "The sun hits the water every day about this time, reflecting into my living room." She used two pull chains. The first drew the vertical Venetians across the glass; the second chain angled them closed.

"The way I see it," I said, watching her walk slowly back to the couch, "it's possible, if not likely that someone from those days killed your father. Someone who wanted to be sure the details of certain weapons deals didn't come out."

"Could be." She sat back down, again curling her legs onto the cushion. "But I don't believe it, all that's back at least ten years. Anyone concerned about that stuff would've killed Papa a long time ago. I'm telling you Clarice killed him for the oldest of reasons, money."

"I way I hear it, your dad called your brother in the middle of the night to tell him he planned to cut Clarice out of his will, and then your brother called you. Is this right?"

"Yes. That was the call I told you I got from him just after the club closed."

"Your brother still lives here in town, right?"

"A few miles from here, on Ocean Boulevard, I can give you the address?"

"I have it."

Susan escorted me to the door where she moved in close. "Have you been coming on to me, Mr. Kile?"

"Whatever made you think that, Ms. Talmadge?"

"Susan."

"Whatever made you think that, Susan?"

"The interest you and Willie were taking in my bathing suit. Would you like to come onto me, Mr. Kile?"

I moved back one step. "I'm trying to do my job."

"I don't know if I was all that helpful, but hopefully I improved your working conditions."

"Yes you did, and I thank you for that."

She stepped forward, erasing my step back and held my gaze with her own. "Unlike my stepmother, I'm not married." Then she kissed me, not the grab-and-squeeze kind, more gentle, our bodies touching, but she kept her hands on my shoulders.

"What are you doing?" I asked.

"Failing, if you can't recognize what I'm doing."

"Why?"

"I like you."

"Everybody likes everybody when they're kissing."

She slowly moved her hand down my arm and brought it around to a more central location. My body rose to meet her.

"Been a while, eh, Mr. Kile?"

I decided not to mention my celibacy calendar. "Matt. Please."

"Been a while, eh, Matt?"

There was no need to answer her.

Chapter 7

CHARAXUS TALMADGE, KNOWN as Charles, lived in a more modern, taller building than the one in which his sister lived. He lived on the eighth floor. I walked past the elevator and took the stairs.

Before I pressed the bell, the door opened with Charles Talmadge holding the inside knob. We stood like two boxers center ring, without a referee to warn us about low blows. He was wearing silver-rimmed dark glasses with reflective lenses. I don't trust people who totally hide their eyes.

His swarthy complexion and attitude gave him just the right look to attract the ladies who favored bad boys. He was wearing a beige linen sport coat, black-pleated lightweight slacks, a black and tan tie, and a white silk shirt. When he stepped forward, tan silk socks peaked out over tasseled black-patent loafers. It was a fashion plate outfit except for his eyes. They were dark to go with his black-wavy hair, but somehow they were not matched, like holes in a working man's boot.

"You didn't need to dress up on my account," I said, scoring the first low blow.

"I don't like your manners, Mr. Kile."

"They could likely use some improvement. I keep working on them, but so far they haven't gotten much better, maybe even a little worse."

"I was on my way out when Susan called to say you'd be here in five minutes. I told her I'd wait, although I see nothing to be gained by our talking."

Free weights and a pressing bench filled the area the developer had designed to be the dining room. The left cut of his sport coat lumped slightly, indicating he was right-handed.

His answers, laboring under a self-imposed gag order, were short and gift-wrapped in surliness. Despite the tough act designed to intimidate, my read was that, except when watching Sponge Bob reruns, most encounters intimidated him. The act was all he had.

Our first few minutes together had gone nowhere and had gotten there fast. "You know who I am and why I'm here," I said, trying to pick up the pace. "I work for the attorney representing your stepmother."

"That bitch. She made a great piece of ass. I don't fault Papa for that, but a wife? Not on her best day. Papa had a great wife, but he left her in France. This bitch was the new, younger version, but Papa wised up. He told both Susan and me that he planned to axe her ass. Kick her down to their prenup. She found out and knocked him off."

"That's not true. Garson told you. You told Susan."

"Same thing."

Far from it, pal. Generally he was saying the same things that Susan had said in her more stylish and respectable manner. I figured they had rehearsed.

He had not yet formally invited me in, but he had retreated far enough to reach around me and push his door shut.

"Listen, Charaxus —"

"Charles, to you, Charlie to my friends, and you aren't one of them."

"Okay, Charles it is. Your stepmother didn't kill your father. I'm trying to find out who did. You oughta want that. Okay if I sit down?"

"The cops have his killer. In lockup she'll sell her ass for much smaller rewards." He pressed his right palm against my chest. Using his right hand was a mistake. He couldn't reach his weapon. Then he said, "Time for you to go," and pushed.

I grasped his hand and twisted hard, levering his thumb toward his wrist. "I didn't say you could touch me. You need to ask your sister for some lessons on how to treat visitors." He winced, bending at the knees to slacken the pressure. I twisted harder. "Drop the tough guy act. You look silly and it won't work." I let go of his thumb.

He flexed his right hand then slid it inside his jacket. I put the flat of my hand over his hand which by now was over his holstered gun, then drove with my legs the way I had in my younger days pushing defenders off the line of scrimmage. He stopped when his backside hit the closed front door. His dark glasses fell to the floor. I put my other forearm against his throat and leaned into it. I also put my foot on top of his glasses.

"I said, drop the tough guy act. You're no good at it. Maybe it worked when you had your daddy's rep backing you up. Now you're just a silly pup trying to play with men."

"Okay. Okay." His shoulders slumped in childlike defiance. "Whatdaya wanna know?"

"For openers, where were you the night your father was killed?"

"I was at home most of the night. I was here when Papa called, and when I called Susan."

"How do you prove that?"

"I think it goes like this: you have to prove I wasn't."

I pushed my arm harder against his throat. Then he said, "A couple people saw me around. I drove to a gym to work out around ten. Then I stopped at the liquor store on the corner of Carson and Atlantic to get some beer."

"What about later?" I asked.

"I met some friends at six for breakfast."

"That doesn't tie it all down does it?"

"Hey. It was just another night. I wasn't into alibi building. God bless America, I'm innocent until proven guilty."

I took my arm from his throat, thrust my hand inside his jacket and pulled out his short-barrel Smith & Wesson. After yanking out his silk shirt tail and using it to wipe my prints off the handle, I held the barrel and tossed the gun behind a chair in the far corner of the room. While I did that he picked up his glasses. When he saw they were broken, he threw them against the far wall. I shoved him toward his dark-brown leather couch and sat on an ottoman fronting the matching chair in the corner.

"Why would your dad call you in the middle of the night to tell you his plans?"

"Papa was impulsive. Once he made a decision, he wanted to kick it into gear."

"Your sister said your father used the two of you in his weapons deals." Susan hadn't actually said this, but I wanted to try out the idea to see if he would disagree. He didn't do so right off, so I carried the idea forward. "She said, you were muscle, I would guess with some real muscle along to back your play. And Garson used your sister to tantalize the men's eyes. Sex and violence, a winning combination, and he kept it all in the family. What a dad. That would also explain your recent trips to France."

Charles wasn't about to offer much so I kept making some educated guesses designed to either get confirmation through his not challenging them, or learn something if he did.

"Lots of children work in the family business. As for Susan, there are guys all over Europe spanking their monkeys with thoughts of my sister. Dad always said, 'Whatever it takes. Get the deal done. There's too much money at stake to be squeamish.' Not that I didn't help with a few wives now and again, while Sis worked the husbands."

"Now, now, gentlemen don't kiss and tell."

He smiled; actually it was more of a snigger.

"There's no percentage in you lying about your dad's late night call. Clarice's attorney will get the phone records."

"I figured somebody, likely the cops, would want verification so I called and got my cell phone company to show me where I needed to go online to see and print a copy of my calls since the last billing," he said. "May I get up? I'll get it for you." I nodded. "It shows both my outgoing and incoming calls."

He handed it to me and sat back down.

Damn. There it was, just like he said. We had expected it would be, but seeing it still had a deflating affect. Garson had called his son a little before two-thirty the morning that someone punched his ticket. After that Charles had called his sister, just like Susan had said.

"I'll need that back. The cops may still want a copy."

"They'll get their own from the source." Fidge probably already knew what I had just confirmed. My old partner was way ahead of me.

"Your last trip to Europe," I said, "closing a deal or bringing somebody into line?"

"That trip was all about pleasure, Mr. Kile, pure pleasure."

"Oh, come on. A handsome fella like you should be able to find lots of females that prefer the bad boy type without having to fly to France."

"She's an old friend. I'd give you her name, but it's none of your business. Papa quit running guns nearly fifteen years ago, five years before we permanently moved to the U.S."

For the fifteen years part of his story to be true, the dynamic duo of sister pussy and brother pain would have been flourishing during their mid-to-late teens and into their early twenties. I'm guessing that Susan could turn a man's head during those ages. But Charles, muscle at that age? No way. Even now Charles wasn't tough enough to scramble a man's eggs.

"Just so we're clear, Charlie, I don't believe your father called you to tell you he planned to drop Clarice from his will. You understand what I'm saying?"

"Sure, that you're entitled to your opinion. Both my sister and I will testify differently, and the attorney will testify he had set up an appointment after my father called to say he wanted to change his will. So, your opinion won't mean shit."

"Your mother's Iraqi. What's her name?"

"I never knew. Sis says Papa told her once, but she doesn't recall."

I parried with the punk for another ten minutes without learning the full depth of his shallowness. I considered bouncing him off a few walls. He would've cracked like a raw egg, but it wasn't the time for that. Not yet. I needed to know more first. I also needed to think about how my doing so might compromise the man I was working for, Brad Fisher.

On the way back to my place my cell rang. It was Rose, my oldest daughter. "What's this I see in the paper about you helping defend this woman, Clarice Talmadge?"

"Yes. I am," I said while turning at the light and heading back toward Long Beach proper.

"Are you sure you want to get back into investigation work?"

"No. I'm not sure. But I felt compelled to do so in this instance."

"Then it's true."

"What?"

"That woman was with you that night. I saw her on TV. She's a beauty, although that's not what Mother called her."

"Oh. And what was that?"

"Mom said the woman must be a badge bunny. Mother told me she was a badge bunny when she met you. She also said you were too old now to be behaving like that, that you should know better."

"She did, eh?" I was nearing my building so I pulled to the curb so as not to risk my phone dropping the call when I pulled into the underground garage. "Rose, for your information I hope I'm never too old to behave that way. But it was nothing like what you're suggesting."

"Mother sounded jealous when she said it, too."

"It's been ten years. You mother and I are not getting back together."

"Which of us are you trying to convince, Father? And, yes, I told mother that as well when she said pretty much the same thing to me earlier."

"Can I go, now, dear?"

"Have a good evening, father. I love you."

"I love you, too, Rose."

Chapter 8

IF BIGAMY WERE legal, I'd have stood right beside Fidge at his wedding and we would have both married Brenda, but bigamy isn't legal, so Brenda became Mrs. Fidgery. Besides when they were wed I had already been married and had two daughters. As for Brenda, truth was I mostly loved her cooking, that and her personality. She could be a bit dirty-mouthed at times, but never in front of her kids, and never in a meanspirited fashion. She just loved to laugh and had a raunchy side that made me smile just to think about.

Fidge had already dropped his son off at Little League practice. Their daughter, Becky, had spent Saturday night at a girlfriend's house for a slumber party, a staple of Americana. The girls were at the age where they would still be sleeping after staying up half the night whispering about which boys at school were the cutest.

I'm not sure at what age females learn the word cute, but it is a decidedly female word. Men do not say cute. Maybe when referring to puppies or new born babies if the guy is in mixed company. There are differences you know between the sexes despite what the modern folks say, and cute is one of those differences. Have you ever heard a man say, "Oh, that dress looks cute on you?" No way. Cute is not a guy word. We may not have a lot that is left to us as pure guy stuff, but not saying *cute* is one of our oases.

Brenda had made pancakes and eggs and bacon, and fresh tomato juice in a mean-looking machine that got me to imagining how it might be used to encourage some thug to confess. Without their kids to help, the three of us would never finish all the food, but it was a grand feast, the kind made doubly good through being shared with the best of friends.

"My old man deals with his boss, Two Dicks, all week," Brenda said, walking toward me. "When you come around, I get to deal with my own version of Two Dicks. How's it hanging Matthew?"

Like Fidge, Brenda called me Matthew. Probably because that's the way she had always heard her husband refer to me. I kissed her on the lips, a peck, and hugged her, a brief closeness that answered her question.

She raised her eyebrows and said, "Yum Yum."

Like I said, Brenda had a raunchy sense of humor. And, like I said, I loved it. She was fun.

We chatted until we were all stuffed. Mostly talk of our respective families and some about my writing. Over coffee, we talked politics hoping the subject didn't cause us indigestion. We talked about the war and immigration, but mostly about how our elected officials, having mismanaged so much of the federal budget for so long, were now trying to right the ship by squeezing Social Security and cutting back on Medicare. None of us were seniors yet, but wrong is still wrong.

Then Brenda broke up the table chatter.

"Why don't you boys go on in the den so you can talk your serious shit. I need to clean up in here anyway." She refilled our coffee cups and headed for the kitchen sink after

Fidge gave her a love swat on her backside. Brenda was a man's woman. She looked back and said, "Later, after the company leaves, before the kids get home."

Just before we walked out of the room, she hiked her house dress halfway up her thighs, pinning it against the front of the counter. "Matthew," she said, "I told the kids to be home by two, so don't you be taking up all our time." She wiggled her ass to punctuate her message. She did have great legs, particularly in the eyes of a man in my condition.

In the den, Fidge pulled the door shut. "Brad Fisher is defending Clarice Talmadge, right?"

I nodded.

"You know, Fisher's tight with Two Dicks."

"What?"

"Their mothers are lifelong gal pals. The two families get together from time to time."

"This situation just keeps getting better and better," I said while shaking my head.

"Well, Matthew, by now you've likely learned that the reputed late night phone calls between the victim and his kids happened. The old guy had planned to put his wife out to pasture."

"The first part, sure," I said, before taking a heat-checking sip of my coffee. "The calls happened, but Susan got it second-hand from her brother, not from her father."

Fidge took a half pint of brandy from a drawer and added a jigger's worth to his coffee. He pointed the bottle toward me. I held up my cup. He poured again.

"Have you checked on the two kids' stories about where they were?"

"Yeah. Although, they aren't exactly suspects."

"They could graduate. Did they check out?"

"Susan's is airtight. Charles is a bit loose, but it would have to run like a Swiss watch for him to be the places we confirmed he was, plus driving time, and get over to knock off his daddy."

"So Charles is unlikely, but possible."

"It would be reaaaal tight. You know, Matthew, we've never been on opposite sides of a case before. It do seem odd."

I moved my head back and forth like a slow motion Kobe Bryant fake before going up for a jumper. "No big deal. We both want the killer put away, that puts us on the same side. We just don't agree on who that is."

"True," Fidge said. "But I got somebody in custody for that role. You don't."

"Not yet, but I'm working on it."

We sat for a minute or two, just sipping. Not sure what to say or not say. Fidge had been right. Things were surely different from how we worked together in the old days.

"I can't believe how your kids have grown," I said finally. "You're getting old, not Brenda, just you."

"It happens, Matthew. So, how much should we tell each other about this case? Problem being we both can expect to eventually be on the stand, not that we haven't fudged on our testimony a time or two in the past."

I smiled. "Anything you say to me that is off the record, I will never repeat to anyone whether or not I'm swore in."

Fidge nodded. "Same here, however, that could mean we may not be able to use stuff if we'd have to disclose the other was the source, even if using it would help our position. In the end, all that means is that we'll each officially know only what we would have known without what we tell each other, if we hadn't opened up."

"I agree, even without asking you to explain what the hell you just said." We laughed and clanked our beverage containers, making our agreement in the way real men had been doing since the beginning of beverage containers.

"Okay, then," Fidge said. "Now that we have that out of the way, let's get to work."

We talked for about an hour and it turned out Fidge had very little I didn't know, and I had nothing he didn't know other than that the kids' mother was Iraqi. The cops had sworn statements from Charles and Susan, with the phone records in support. Fisher and I had expected all that. They also had three neighbors ready to testify about Garson and Clarice arguing loudly for days. That was no surprise. Several wives were eager to testify about Clarice and their husbands, although from my way of looking at it the husbands had made their own decisions and were equally wrong. Still, the most widely held view in our society said women on the make were not supposed to bark up another women's tree. Clarice's prints were not on the murder weapon, explanation: she used the scarf. The cops were betting that not many could scale the outside of the building to reach the Talmadge's fourth floor balcony, and there were no clawing marks on the balcony edge or railing. Fidge admitted that position was flimsy, that a killer could come up the outside using a padded grappling hook and basic rope-climbing skills.

The killer coming in that way, however, from what was known, could not exit that same way. It would be impossible to close the door behind him to two inches and make it to the rail without leaving an exit footprint. The killer could have left using a key taken from inside the house, but Garson's key was in his pocket and Clarice's key was in her purse. In her statement, Clarice had said the household had no spare key. As for other keys, the building had tight key control, and all keys had been accounted for. Fidge also made me say again that I never had a key to the Talmadge condo.

This line of thinking led us to the obvious, if the killer had somehow gotten a key to aid his exit, then he would not have needed the Ninja bit on the outside wall to get in. This take on it made the zigzag footprint on the deck unrelated to the murder.

Fidge confirmed he had not found a shoe with the sole print pattern that matched the balcony footprint and had been unable to tie it to any building workman or service provider. He didn't see that print as much of anything. It remained a loose end which meant it would be hard for either the defense or prosecutor to make much out of it. The mystery of it could help Fisher if he could tie in something else suggestive of an outside killer. I shared my suspicions about the two kids killing their father. Fidge shrugged off all of that. I could see why.

"Matthew, you know your involvement with this dame was going to come out. I had to put it in my report, you know, the part about her claiming to have been with you in your place. Of course, the press got it. This is a sexy story, old guy with millions and a sexy younger wife; the media will shadow us every step of the way."

"I understand. I know you couldn't avoid it." Fidge nodded, his head lowered a bit while he did.

Fidge and I had absorbed all the coffee and brandy and wishful thinking we could. So we broke off our discussions, agreeing we would talk again when one of us had something substantive to share.

I found Brenda in the kitchen baking beer bread. I thanked her for the best breakfast I'd had since, well, since the last time I'd eaten with her family. And she thanked me for leaving a couple of hours before the kids were due home. The woman had an overactive sex drive; although I admit not knowing where the line is that one crosses to be oversexed. But their lovemaking was a good thing. It was about the only aerobic exercise in Fidge's life.

Chapter 9

"SUSAN'S A REAL fox," I said to Brad Fisher while we talked on the phone as I drove home from having breakfast with Fidge and Brenda. "Daddy's efforts to make Charles into an enforcer failed miserably. He doesn't have the spine for it. He'll open up like an oyster, if we ever need to crack our way in."

"What did you find out from the two of them?" Fisher asked.

"Their stories were similar enough to suggest a rehearsal. Susan is a law school grad so she's likely trying to coach her brother, but he's a chauvinist, so he's refusing her direction to some degree. We may be able to play them against one another at some point. The cops have checked their alibis and they seem okay, at least for now."

"So you got nothing heavy duty?"

"Susan confirmed her real mother was Iraqi. Charles Talmadge showed me his cell phone statement to date for the month. He had gone online and printed it. Be prepared, and all that stuff. The call from his dad was there, just like he told the cops. But we were expecting that. So, yeah, I've got nothing heavy duty, but we're only in the second inning."

"I've gotten a copy of the in-and-out calls on Garson Talmadge's phone," Brad said. "The old guy called his son all right. Then he must have turned his phone off, but there was a message later from his daughter. The phone records show the two of them didn't talk before he died."

"Anything significant in her message?"

"No. Just, call me, Papa. We need to talk."

"So that's it?"

"The victim's phone records showed no history of real late calls between Garson and either of his kids. So something out of the ordinary was going on that night."

"Those calls will score for the D.A."

"Hell, those calls are an NBA three-pointer," Brad said while I turned onto Ocean Boulevard. "The jury will assume family calls that time of night to have been about something big, like a decision to change a will. Anyway, we can't do much about any of that. You need to find me something that will call his kids' veracity into question, particularly the son because Susan didn't actually talk to her father."

"Like the song says, right now, *I got plenty of nothin'*. Maybe a few feelings I can't square in my mind."

"Such as?"

"Garson must've been a cold-blooded son of a bitch to raise his son to be muscle in the dangerous world of weapons deals. Charles also said something about the old man using Susan to seduce customers, offer bribes or curry favors in some fashion. What father would do that?" Saying it was like having a piano fall on me, but Brad said it first.

"What if he's not their father?"

"That's just what I was thinking," I said. "We got no reason to question he is, other than you'd have to be a class-A prick to use your kids that way."

"How do we find out?"

"I'd like your okay to go to Europe — France, to start. But first I need to find some names and addresses over there, somebody who might know something. If his death is a carryover from his gun running days, the answers are over there, not here."

"I've got a copy of Garson's immigrations application," Brad said. "It came in by courier late Friday, also his ten-year-old citizenship application. A glance is all I've taken so far. There was one address in France, don't recall whose. Sappho and Charaxus are definitely shown as his children, I did notice that. They came over with him."

"You at the office?" I asked.

"At home."

"You got an hour? Let's meet at your office. Let me get a look at that stuff. I might find a French connection."

"I can be there in twenty," Brad said. "I can't stay long. My in-laws are coming over for a late-afternoon barbeque."

We were about to hang up when Fisher paused the way people do when they are deciding whether or not to say something more. Then he did. "I'm going to see Clarice tomorrow at noon. It's mostly technical legal mumbo-jumbo. But in light of this discussion, I'd like you there as well. I have never spoken to her about France, Garson's ex, the background on his two kids, all that stuff. Have you and she ever talked about any of that?"

"Not a word."

"Well, before we send you off to France, we should. Women rarely marry a man who has been married previously without asking about the prior marriage, any kids, where they lived, like that. Gals are different from guys that way. Europe, even France is a big place without something to point you somewhere."

"I'll come by your office at eleven in the morning. We'll go together. We can kick it around some more on the way."

"I'm expecting a copy of Garson's will tomorrow morning, also the prenuptial. They should arrive before you do. Now, let's get moving, my wife's folks remember."

"See you in twenty minutes. We'll be done in time for your barbeque. Take some pictures. I'd love to see how you look in an apron, maybe one of those tall chef's hats. A red scarf would be a nice touch, or perhaps a wine sommelier's pewter saucer on a chain around your neck."

"You are a writer, aren't you?"

We hung up listening to each other laugh.

Forty minutes later, I drove up the embankment from the underground parking in Brad Fisher's building. On the car seat beside me lay a folder holding copies of Garson's immigration and citizenship papers. On both documents, Garson had listed a Paris address. At the time Garson applied to come here on a temporary basis he had listed the address as his home. Years later, when applying for citizenship, he had listed the same address as his home before coming to America. Maybe his ex-wife, Chantal, still lived there. Odds said no, but maybe the French were less transient than modern Americans. Brad's staff had been unable to come up with a phone number for the ex.

We were hoping Clarice would point me in some clearer direction.

Chapter 10

SOMETIME LATE LAST night, or early this morning, the fog had again sailed into Long Beach like a silent armada. Only, unlike the armadas of history, nature's invading force had proceeded ashore to bring together cars that were otherwise trying to avoid each other. The damp shroud blanketed everything that existed within its domain.

As I approached the front of Brad Fisher's building, the morning sun had burned off enough of the fog to bring into view the blurry red, then green traffic light at the next intersection.

Brad and I got to the jail a few minutes before ten. On the short drive out, I asked Brad about his relationship with Captain Richard Dickson. Fidge had gotten it right, pretty much anyway. The two men's mothers had been very close for sixty years. More like sisters than friends. Out of respect, each of the men called the other's mother, aunt. Brad knew about the men in blue calling Captain Dickson, Two Dicks. When I said it, Brad smiled like he understood.

A youngish officer with a crew cut, wearing a tightly filled guard shirt and highly-polished boots, the kind with toes hard enough to drop a recalcitrant inmate to his knees jerked his head toward a hallway and then walked that direction. We followed his head nod, assuming it meant he would escort us to our client. He did.

Clarice looked a bit better than when I saw her the last time. More resigned to her situation, accepting of it, deflated. Deflated better described her state of mind than accepting of it. Even her boobs appeared lower. I didn't think that could happen with implants. Maybe the sag was just part of the going-nowhere-doing-nothing-incarceration slouch with which I was all too familiar.

The guard put us in one of the jail's private rooms reserved for lawyers and clients to plan their strategies. Nothing sneaky, of course, no conniving, of course, everything legal, of course, just good old-fashioned, honest-to-goodness lawyering.

If people are presumed innocent until proven guilty, why are they held in jail pending trial? Why do they need to post bail, when bail is allowed, so they can get out? Until convicted, they're supposed to be presumed innocent of all charges, aren't they? If so, they should be able to walk right out, subject to a legal obligation to show up for trial. I know. I know. The overwhelming majority, being guilty as charged, would find a hole somewhere or skip the country. But the point is if they are presumed innocent, why don't they have the right to find a nice warm hole or to expatriate themselves? Innocent and free should go together, shouldn't it? I've always wondered about that. As a cop it never troubled me because the ones Fidge and I arrested, we knew were guilty. The only question being whether some silver-tongued shyster would twist the very rules of justice against justice or, in the end, befuddle the jury sufficiently to make them see reasonable doubt — or at least its shadow.

Clarice's personality also seemed flatter, were bosoms and attitudes somehow related? Then again, anyone would get down staying in a cold, sad place filled with the sounds and smells of fear, not to mention gas and unwashed armpits.

She sat down. More like plopped down in a scarred wooden chair and lazily crossed her arms resting them more on her lap than the plumping position where she normally held them. She had little to say in reply to Brad's comments and questions regarding the legal proceedings. Her yes and no answers often expressed with a movement of her head rather than her mouth. That is they were until we started discussing what she recalled about Garson's time in Europe and his ex-wife. Not that her spirit perked up, her answers just necessarily got longer.

"My guess is his ex … Charlene, I think," she began.

"Chantal," I corrected, taking a seat in the remaining chair. I had remained standing while Brad and she had been discussing the legal mumbo-jumbo, as Brad had characterized it.

"Yeah. That's it, Chantal," Clarice said, "a classy name don't you think? My guess, I don't know, you understand, but my guess is she'd still be there. Every month Garson sent a check over to pay a lot of her bills. He never mentioned her moving. Then again, he never really talked about her much after we got married. As part of their divorce Tally had agreed to pay that stuff for Chantal and her sister, as long as either of them lived. He wanted to be free of her before he applied for U.S. citizenship. He also gave her a big wad of cash on the front end."

"How did he feel about having to put out all that money?" Fisher asked, loudly scooting his metal chair back on the cement flooring. My non-matching chair had wooden legs.

Clarice's chair was more like Brad's only those two didn't match either.

"It pissed him off to no end," Clarice said. "Tally would rant and rave about how she had him over the barrel at the time. He wanted a quickie divorce, while she was in no hurry. The way he tells it, she bled him before giving in."

"His will," I said, having read it quickly before leaving Brad's office, "showed a trust fund would be established to be sure those payments continued as long as Chantal lived, or her sister, Camille Trenet, lived."

"I don't think," Fisher said, "I've ever known of a divorce agreement and will that provided, even on a contingent basis, payments to a spouse's siblings."

"That is odd," I said, as if my observation added something substantive.

"Tally wasn't a benevolent man," Clarice said, "not in the slightest. So, when he told me about that one night, after a few bottles of wine, I figured his ex knew something heavy duty. My opinion at the time was there was more involved than simply Tally's desire for a quick divorce. I mean, he didn't really need to be divorced first, at least I don't think he did. He just wanted to be before entering the U.S."

Right then, something slammed against the wall outside the door. I assumed our escort's steel toed boots had been put to use. The noise settled down and we continued our discussion.

"Okay," Brad said, taking a blank legal pad from his case. "Let's talk about some new things. Tell us everything you know about his two kids."

"What's to tell? One boy, one girl, both adults, at least as to age. Susan's an intelligent, beautiful and poised woman. She can handle herself anywhere in any company. Charlie is an empty suit."

That had been my assessment as well. If the fast food restaurants sold men, he would have been the ninety-nine-cent special.

"He tries to be tough," Clarice said, continuing her answer. "Tally pushed him that way. I don't know why. But Charlie just doesn't have it. Call his bluff and he fades. Not a bad looking guy, if you don't mind his lack of brains and balls. Still, he did do some strong arm work for his father, but he always took along a couple of bonafide bouncer types when he did. He used to brag about it some, trying to puff up his image, little comments that always drew stern shut-up looks from his father."

"And this was after the three of them moved to the U.S.?" I asked.

"Oh, sure," she said. "I didn't meet Tally until after they came stateside."

"So these activities continued after that?"

"Yes. The most recent time was about a year and a half ago."

"You know, they're claiming your husband planned to cut you out of his will," Brad said. "Drop you back to the prenup. Do you think Garson would do that?"

"Probably. But Tally is the type that would have told me the next time he got angry. And Lord knows the man got angry lots the last few days. So, no, I don't think so. He would have thrown it in my face and he didn't."

"Maybe he just decided that night," Brad said, "just before he called Charlie. That would have left him no time to gloat."

"Possible," Clarice admitted. "Anything's possible, but the order is still wrong." Brad and I looked at her inquisitively. She clarified. "He would first bounce it off Susan, not Charlie. Tally knew she was the smart one. My husband respected brains. His son always found things out later, mostly after the decision had been made."

"He did call Charles," Brad said. "We have the phone records."

"Then," Clarice replied, "he called Charlie about something else, something routine."

"Routine at two-thirty in the morning? Or whatever time it was," I said. "That doesn't seem the time for a routine call."

"I don't know," Clarice said. "But I do know he never called Charles to talk about important stuff. Even when he thought he had made up his mind, he'd say, 'I wanna hear Susan's thoughts on this before I do it.'"

Brad and I looked at each other. It wasn't that we didn't believe her. Then I said, "What she's saying fits with my take on the two kids."

"I don't doubt you, Matt, but that won't cancel out the picture the DA'll paint for the jury using those phone records and the kids' testimonies."

Brad looked hard into Clarice's eyes. "Is Garson their father?"

Clarice didn't move except for her eyes getting wider. The question was too plain to be misunderstood. For a good part of a minute, she stared back and forth between Brad and me. "Golly. Wow," she finally said. "Where did that come from?"

"Okay. The question surprised you, but answer it," I said. We waited, listening to the hum from a wounded light ballast, the only sound in the windowless room.

"He said so," she began. "I had no reason to think otherwise. If not, he never told me. Why?"

"The prosecution will present a loving father and two children. Then you come along and marry the old man for his money. They'll trot out the wives in the building to testify about your doing their husbands, also that you and the deceased fought regularly near the end. Then Garson wises up and calls his attorney screaming, 'I'm going to change my will.' Before he can, he's killed. Juries, being parents themselves, don't want to think kids kill their papas for money. Somehow we need to tip over that cart. Setting children up as alternative suspects is dicey, but if we can just tarnish the kids a little, make them less likeable, it could help a lot."

Clarice just sat there. Maybe for the first time getting a clear look at the mess she was in.

"Brad needs to discredit as much of that as possible," I said. "Garson hadn't told his attorney how he wanted to change his will. We can expect the jury to assume he planned to cut you out. Why? A man wouldn't cut his children out of his will. Would he? Maybe he would, if they weren't his kids."

Clarice tugged on the fabric of her jail suit. Then she crossed her legs, without being provocative, although it was hard for Clarice to do anything without ringing man-bells.

"They have the phone records and Garson's attorney's testimony," Brad said, picking up where I had left off. "I need to be able to knock some of that off kilter. Matt here will be working hard at finding out more about Susan and Charles. Also, about Garson's gun running. What can you tell us about that?"

Clarice shrugged. "He always insisted he was out of that business, not that I completely believed him."

"Why didn't you completely believe him?" I asked.

"He would get some really serious phone calls, from Susan mostly. They'd talk French. I couldn't follow any of it, except that I could tell it was serious shit. Also, Charlie sometimes flew to France."

"What about Susan?" I asked.

"I don't recall her going to Europe. But she drove up to L.A., I don't think Garson knew she did that."

"How did you?"

"She came by one day, just before lunch. Tally took her out on the balcony to talk, and their conversation was very animated. I stuck my head out to say I was going shopping. I drove up to Enterprise, just a few blocks, left my wheels and rented a car. I followed her."

"Why would you do that?" Brad asked.

"Curiosity mostly, I don't know, maybe they just talked in private when I was there one too many times. Maybe I was just being melodramatic. I started wondering what Sue did with her days. By the way, she hates being called Sue so don't do that unless you're trying to piss her off. Anyway, after she left college, I expected she'd take a job, but she didn't. Tally always gave her, both of 'em, plenty of money. Susan was appreciative; Charlie always wanted more. Truth was they were both capable of supporting themselves, especially Susan. That's when I started figuring Tally had gone back to moving weapons, if he had ever stopped. Over time I just got fed up with the way he and his kids would look at each other and then talk French when I was around. That morning, my curiosity just got the best of me. I tailed her."

"And?" We asked, nearly in concert.

"Susan drove up to L.A. out near U.C.L.A. on the west side. She parked in a lot near the Medical Center. By the time I got parked, I lost her in the busy Westwood shopping area. I was about to give up when I caught a glimpse of her rounding the corner onto Wilshire Boulevard. I'm not all that familiar with that neighborhood. I can't recall whether she turned left or right on Wilshire."

"What time of day was that?" I asked.

"By then, I'd say mid-afternoon, twoish."

"When you saw her walking around the corner onto Wilshire," I said, "was the sun at her back or in her face?"

"It was high," Clarice said. "I can't really say in which direction in relation to Susan. No. Wait a minute. When I got to the corner and looked up Wilshire in the direction she had gone, I had to squint because the sun was in my face. But I never saw her on Wilshire after she turned. By then she would have been more than a block ahead."

"She was headed west," I said, "into the setting sun. That's why you had to squint."

I didn't say anything in front of Clarice, but the FBI Field Office for the greater Los Angeles area was on Wilshire not too far west from where Susan had turned the corner. What that meant, I had no idea. Odds were it meant absolutely nothing. There were many other stores and offices in that same direction.

I switched the subject again. "Garson's ex-wife, is she French? The kids appear to have some Middle Eastern in them. What can you tell me about the mother?"

"Tally didn't say a lot. I mean, like I said before, he told me he had a French ex-wife, not an Arab wife. That he paid her off and got his divorce."

"Was he married before her?"

"I don't know. I don't think so."

"Were Susan and Charles her children? The French wife's," Brad said to clarify his question.

"I've been to France," I said, "a few times. There are a lot of Middle Easterners in France. She could be a French citizen of Middle Eastern descent."

"That would cover the ethnicity," Brad said, "but she could have been given the French name, Chantal, despite her Iraqi origin."

"Susan didn't recall her mother's name," I said for Clarice's benefit, "but she did say Garson had told her that her mother was Iraqi." I paused to engage her eyes. "How come Garson had a typewriter? I mean, hardly anybody has one these days, particularly if they also have a computer."

"He watched some movie where they mined a guy's computer to find even the stuff he had deleted. After that Tally went out and bought a used typewriter."

"When does he use it?" Brad asked.

"For personal correspondence, at least that's what he says. I can't be certain. He keeps that stuff to himself."

Before we left, Brad brought up the media conjecture about Clarice having been at my place the night Garson had been killed. "We may have to think about changing detectives." He looked at me, "You understand, Matt?"

I nodded. I did. But Clarice would have none of it.

"No way," she said. "No change. That's final. Matt knows how to investigate homicides. He knew Tally and he knows me. There'd be too much slippage to bring a new one up to date and I would never trust anyone else like I do Matt."

"For now," Brad said, "fine. But we may need to visit this again."

When we were back in Brad's car, he said, "It's time for you to rack up some frequent flyer miles."

"First," I said, "I'll go see Susan. I've got Clarice's dog, Asta. Susan likes Asta so I'll drop the mutt off with her. Maybe I can learn something more before I leave for France. Garson and the kids were with that ex-wife until they came to America. Susan ought to be able to clear up the confusion between her saying her mother was an Iraqi, and her father's ex, a woman she had to know as a child, being named Chantal. However, none of this establishes these two women are not one in the same, an Iraqi woman with a French name."

"I don't think so," Brad said. "Garson and his kids were in France long enough that if his ex and the kid's Iraqi mother were one in the same, Susan would have said her mother's name was Chantal, not some Iraqi name she couldn't recall."

"Makes sense," I said. "But let's hear what Susan has to say about that, and then try for corroboration in France."

Chapter 11

I CALLED SUSAN Talmadge who eagerly agreed to take custody of Asta for a few days. My flight left at ten on Tuesday morning, so at seven Monday night I dropped Asta off at Susan's upstairs condo near Cherry Beach.

"It's nice to see you again, Matt Kile," Susan said as soon as she opened the door. She took the lucky dog into her arms. I was envious, but I turned and went back down to the car to get the dog's dish and sleeping pillow, a nearly full bag of dry food and a box of doggie treats. The whole thing made me feel domestic.

When I came back up the stairs, Asta had her nose against the screen, her excited feet tap dancing on the tile insert just inside the door, her tail keeping time with the dance tune only Asta heard. After I stepped inside, the pouch dashed down the hall to check out her new digs. Susan was in the kitchen, from where I heard a high-speed light motor. A moment later the dog passed through the living room heading toward the kitchen likely to search out the floor spot where she expected her dog dish would soon be located.

I sat down on the long couch just as Susan came in carrying a pitcher of blended Margaritas. That explained the whirling sound I had heard. In her other hand she held two glasses. She put all that on the coffee table next to a clear glass plate crowded with crackers and slices of cheese, precut to fit the crackers. "I haven't had a chance yet to pick up any Irish, I hope these margaritas will substitute?"

"I love margaritas, thank you."

"You look tired, have you eaten anything?" she asked.

"I scrambled two eggs this morning, nuked some bacon and washed it down with some Irish."

"Would you like something more? I could light the BBQ and make us a burger?"

After some more back and forth about food and my inappropriate choice of Irish as a morning juice, I convinced her margaritas and cheese and crackers would be enough. I hadn't been expecting even that.

She had not put on her yellow bikini, but looked just as delicious in an orange halter top with a plunging rounded neckline, perfectly complemented by the rich tan of her smooth skin. Below the top was a pair of beige linen shorts, gathered in the front by a drawstring bow. Gold sandals gripped her feet that had nails painted to match her orange top.

"Is this the treatment your father trained you to give his customers?"

"No, Matt, this is a woman showing interest in a man. Do you have a problem with that?"

"Not for a minute. I'm flattered."

"Good. You said you'd have a few questions when you dropped off Asta."

"Susan, can I ask you something right off? Actually, I have to; it's part of my investigation."

"Let's have it."

"You told me that your mother was Iraqi, but that you didn't recall her name."

"That's right."

Asta, having finished checking out the house, came over to Susan and licked the orange polish on her toes. Susan smiled and wiggled her foot, but didn't shoo Asta away.

I fought off being jealous of Asta, and asked, "You and your brother lived in France for several years with your dad and his French wife, Chantal?"

"Yes. I liked Chantal. She was fun, but Papa divorced her and we came to America. I haven't seen or heard from Chantal since. She took the divorce hard."

"Then Chantal is not your mother?"

"Oh, no. But we thought of her like she was our mother until Papa told us we were going to America and we were never again to speak of Chantal. Our real mother was Iraqi. We never knew anything about her until I was about ten. Papa told us he had been close to our mother during his business trips to Iraq. That he loved her, even though at the time he was married to Chantal."

"What happened to your birth mother? Do you know?"

"She died giving us birth. You know, medical care for childbirth is not so good there. Papa said he told Chantal about all of that and she accepted us as her children, even though we were not."

"What else do you remember about your mother, or your dad's trips to Baghdad?"

"I only vaguely remember Papa's trips to Iraq. Actually, I'm not sure whether I remember them or just that I've always known he made them. He would just leave. Be gone. Maybe Chantal knew to where, but all we knew was Papa was gone on business. As for our mother, you now know all I know."

Susan refilled our margarita glasses. "Charlie told me you stopped by the other day."

I kept my answer short. If she wanted to talk about my visit with her brother, I wanted her to do most of the talking so I might hear more of what she had been told by Charles.

"Yes, I did."

"He said you were rough on him."

I sat my glass on the table. "Your brother is not the welcoming kind."

Susan laughed. "You got that right. He can be gruff at times."

"Does gruff include pulling a gun?" I took a cheese cracker.

"He told me you took it away from him. Is that true?"

"Yes."

"You fought?"

"A little pushing, that's all."

"Did he tell you what you wanted to know?"

"He told me he called you after his father called him. Is that correct?"

"Yes."

"A few minutes later you called your father to ask if what Charles had just told you was true."

"I'd tell you I called Papa for a different reason, but you'd know that for anything else I would have waited until morning. So, yes, that's why I called Papa that late."

"And?"

"Papa had turned his phone off. I left a message for him to call me. Obviously, he never did."

"Charles told me your father brought him up to be muscle for his business. And, he said, that Garson raised you to be —" I didn't finish the sentence.

"I admit it," she said without much hesitation. "Papa used me to influence men in France from whom he, shall we say, needed favors."

"You must have resented that."

"Not resented. I was confused why he wanted me to do those things. But I came to understand."

"I don't understand your not feeling resentful?"

"He trained me to be a seductress, for lack of a better word. Although, it was not all that often that it went beyond flirting, enticing, teasing. A few dates and some weekend trips, that was part of it, too."

"Why do you think he did that?"

"It was an expected part of his business. I filled out early and the men liked me. I didn't mind being a seductress. Perhaps I would have become one anyway. You understand a seductress is different than a hooker, don't you Matt?"

"I think I do."

"One day I want to marry. The skills Papa brought ladies in to teach me, will allow me to heighten my husband's joys. So, in the end, all I did was have sex with a dozen or so men, that looking back I wish I hadn't. But which woman can look back and not say the same thing?"

"I'm sorry; I still think it's lousy for a father to do that to a teenage daughter, for that matter, for any man to."

"It wasn't all that hard. Once I figured out what men wanted, it got easier."

"And what is it that men want?" I asked.

"Beyond the obvious, they want you to be their mother, or their daughter, maybe their addiction. Which do you want me to be?"

"Not my mother or daughter, or sister or aunt for that matter. I never knew either of my grandmothers that well, so I'm not taking applications to fill that position either. I guess that leaves addiction. But not yet, I've got a case I'm working first. Trouble is, you're part of that case and I don't know what part. Not yet anyway."

Susan chewed her second cheese cracker. I had no idea how swallowing could be sensuous? But when she did, it was. Then she asked, "What I did, for Papa, you know, does that change your impression of me?"

I took another drink before replying. "One thing being a cop taught me, Susan. People from all walks are often quite different than what one might expect. I've met preachers I wouldn't trust to carry the offering to the altar. I've also met some hardworking hookers with a lot of class. Even a burglar who operates under his own moral code. Its where a person is, who they really are, where they're going with their life that matters, not what events in the past that they couldn't control required of them. Now that's as philosophical as I'm going to get."

"I like you Matt Kile. I like what you said. I don't want you to go yet, and I don't want to talk about my Papa's business or my brother's bad manners. Tell me about your family."

Asta came to my side, appearing satisfied with what she had learned during her inspection of the premises, and her sniffing and licking of Susan's feet. The dog touched my hand with her wet nose, and then snuggled up against my shoes. All reasonably intelligent animals sense fear. Dogs sense more. Asta had figured out that I was leaving. Maybe Asta was also feeling lucky, while I was gone she would get to sleep with Susan, at least curl up with her. And probably get to lie on the fluffy bathroom rug while Susan showered.

Damn lucky dog, I thought, before answering Susan's question. "I'm divorced, nearly eight years now. My ex and my two grown children live in Downey. That's about twenty-five miles inland from here."

"How long were you married?"

"Fourteen years. I'm forty-six. My ex is forty-three. We have two daughters."

Susan continued to ask questions about my family and I went on to tell her that my daughters were smart and pretty, and, of course, that I was completely objective in that assessment. Rose, my oldest is twenty-one, dropped out of college and took a job with Farmers and Merchants Bank. She is engaged with a June marriage in the planning. Amy is one year younger, had skipped a year in high school and is attending Harvard, studying accounting, and busy picking between a super brain who is into computer design and a bad-boy biker. You likely know which one I prefer. She's also green with envy over her sister getting married.

"How would you describe things now between you and your ex?"

"After thousands of years of language, there is no word that describes it succinctly. But Good comes close," I said. "We share our children, but that's about it. I wish her well. She feels the same, I think. There'll be no reconciliation. We've grown apart."

Susan stood. "I don't want to keep you too long. I know you fly out in the morning. I'd like to see you when you get back."

"Susan, I owe Brad Fisher, Clarice's attorney, not to mention Clarice herself. I know you don't think much of your stepmother ... that you —"

"Oh, she's not such a bad sort, not really," Susan said. "We're probably more alike than either of us cares to admit. Still, she killed Papa so I can never wish her well."

"If that proves out, I understand. Perhaps we should leave it at that. Goodnight."

"Matt. Let me try to say it better. I want to see you when you get back, not to talk about what you learned. Leave the case in your car before you come upstairs. Okay?"

"I may have more questions I'll need to ask you after I get back."

"I'll be here. Besides, you'll need to come get Asta."

I was half way out the door when I remembered. "Oh," I said while turning back to face her, "another question, sorry." She smiled. "I need names in France, Europe, in the Middle East. Men your dad worked with or for. Men you saw when helping your father."

"You have to understand I was a teenager and in my twenties during that time. Many times Papa just gave me a first name for the men. As I got older I realized the names were not their real names. I wish I could help more."

"You don't remember anyone? Maybe the companies they worked for or their positions in the government."

"Only one, I never had his name, but I saw his picture in the paper a few weeks after Papa had me go away with him for the weekend. I do recall the picture caption identified him as a government official. I want to say an undersecretary in the defense department, that's a translation, of course, also a guess. I doubt this is of any help but it's all I have."

"Would you recognize a picture of him?"

"Maybe. Yeah. I think so."

Susan kissed me on the cheek. "Will you come see me when you get back? Stay longer?"

"I'd have to be statue not to want to. Looking at you makes me think of a fireplace burning on a foggy morning, and drinking fresh-squeezed orange juice while snuggling under a down comforter. But all that will have to wait until this thing is over. Then, should you still want to ... well we'll see."

She leaned in and kissed me on the other cheek, and whispered, "More later."

I left the only suspect from whom I had ever received a kiss on the cheek, let alone a promise of, "more later."

Chapter 12

I STOPPED AT the grocery store and bought a prepaid cell phone and used it to call Malloy. I didn't remember his first name. I had only seen the man once since I got out of jail, when I had needed a duplicate key made. I wasn't sure he was still in business or would admit to remembering me. "Malloy, Matt Kile here. I need your help."

"I told you I'd be here if you ever needed me."

"Not so quick. Let me tell you what's up before you decide."

"I read the papers; I can guess. You know I don't do strong arm stuff so you wouldn't be calling if that's what you needed. Quit beating your gums and get to it."

"You still in the locksmith business?"

"Of course, you're calling me at my shop. I'll be sixty-six early next year so that'll do it for me. I'll sell out then and retire."

"Can you still pick 'em?"

"Like riding a bike, truth is I've gotten better, even picked up a few new tricks. What do you need Matt?"

"I need you to be invisible. I don't want trouble for you."

"I'd likely have gone up for three to five back then, and never had this shop if it hadn't been for you. You took a risk for me. This makes it my turn."

"I meant what I said, Malloy. All sight unseen or you wave it off and go home. It won't do me or you any good if you're seen by anyone."

"I'm closing the shop now. Fifteen minutes, the bench overlooking the beach down near the pier. You know where. Can you make it by then?"

"I'll be there," I said, already heading for my car. "Well, gimme twenty."

Malloy had cracked a safe in a big home on the cliff overlooking the San Pedro harbor, and had gotten away clean. Later when going through the loot, he had found not only a huge amount of cash, but also jewelry that had been taken in a jewelry store holdup a few weeks before, during which a clerk and a customer had been shot dead. The plans for that heist had also been in the safe. Fidge and I had being working that jewelry robbery and murder case for weeks without making even one first down.

We had known Malloy was a burglar. We had also known he abhorred violence and had no respect for those who used violence in burglaries and robberies. Malloy had often given us information he had gleaned in his world about those kinds of crooks — saying they gave the honest business of burglary a bad name.

We never had evidence pinning Malloy to any specific job, but we got to recognize his excellent planning and exacting execution. For this particular case, Malloy anonymously delivered the jewels and plans to the department, to our attention. The note saying he had seen our names in the paper as being in charge of the case. It took us a while to find enough linking that guy to the robbery and murder, but it never would have happened without Malloy pointing us at him. It's not worth rehashing all the details but eventually we were able to build a case and the guy got life for the murders.

The law often lets an arrested criminal go if he can give up something bigger. Other times, the D.A. will plea bargain down to a lesser charge in return for evidence or leads involving a bigger case. So Fidge and I saved the system a lot of time and took it upon ourselves to let Malloy walk. Malloy hadn't bargained to get out of trouble; he had gotten away clean after the safe job. So, we weren't about to jam him up. Malloy retired right after that and we figured used the cash from the safe job to buy the locksmith shop. The jewelry store got back its jewelry, and the jewelry store owner had only included a nominal amount of cash in the list of things stolen. The substantial cash Malloy had gotten from the safe had apparently come from other unknown criminal dealings. So, we had a murdered in jail and had contributed to converting a burglar into an honest small businessman. On balance, it seemed a nice mix of right and wrong.

Malloy had gotten to the beach before me, and was watching the moon glisten off the breakers when I arrived. It took no more than a couple of minutes to let Malloy know what I wanted done and how I wanted it staged.

"Piece of cake, Sergeant," he said, "not a problem."

"I'm not a sergeant anymore."

"To me you always will be."

I gave Malloy the building address and the Talmadge condo number, as well as the location of the building supervisor's office. I also gave him the name of the local reporter I wanted to get the story. The last thing we discussed was the timeline for the job. I wanted it wrapped up and delivered while I was in France.

The next morning, I boarded the plane with the early Long Beach paper under my arm. The lead story was about Clarice Talmadge and her promiscuous behavior. The first paragraph talked about her claiming to have been at my place. That was followed by a brief, but generally accurate account of my career in law enforcement, my justice-on-the-courthouse-steps shooting, and then some about my being a mystery writer. They even mentioned my latest novel, so on balance that was good and the rest was old news. The next few paragraphs quoted one unnamed source that referred to Clarice as an old-fashioned trollop, while another, also hiding behind anonymity called her a harlot. I figured they both lived in my condo building. As a writer I'd have picked a different slur because harlot and trollop are suggestive of a prostitute, and I doubted Clarice ever took payment beyond pleasure. And she gave as much pleasure as she received; in most cases probably gave more and we all know it is better to give than receive.

Chapter 13

MY BRITISH AIRWAYS flight touched down at Charles de Gaulle Airport in Paris a few minutes after noon, local time. My only luggage, a carry-on, was a big leather sports bag which I had bought at an auction. The guy standing next to me while I was bidding said it had once been owned by Tiger Woods. The black bag was one of those with zipper compartments on the ends as well as the big zipper down the center top of the bag. Tiger Woods's bag, eh, so I bid and, given my competitive nature, kept bidding, with the hope that somewhere inside might be a forgotten list of a few of Tiger's ex-girls-on-the-sly, complete with phone numbers. As you've likely already guessed, there was no list, if it had ever been Tiger's bag to begin with. The auction had been to raise money for scholarships for the children of soldiers killed in Middle East conflicts. I'm at peace with the whole thing, even if the shill who kept egging me on to bid again and again remembers me as a chawbacon. I love that word, chawbacon. I don't remember where I first heard it. The dictionary says it's a word to describe a rube, a yokel, a bumpkin, and I had been all of that when I had allowed myself to be led into believing the bag had once been owned by Tiger Woods. But then, everyone active in sports owned at least one sports bag, so, who knows, maybe it had been one of Tiger's. Yeah, okay, I had been a chawbacon.

I sailed through customs with my Tiger bag strapped over my shoulder. At least I did until a female French immigrations officer stepped in front of me. "Your presence is requested in that room." She pointed.

"What is this about? Your immigrations desk found my papers to be in order."

"They will explain, Mr. Kile. Please follow me." She went on ahead and I followed, which was not a wholly unpleasant experience. She opened the door to a small room, looked back and smiled, then walked out of my life. The room was empty. The walls held no pictures. Not even a promotional poster for French champagne. Totally empty other than a small table and three unfriendly chairs, two on one side of the table and one on the other. I dropped my Tiger bag along the wall and sat in the lonelier chair, facing the two empties.

My instincts told me I was being watched. I'd say maybe even videotaped, but that might sound paranoid at this point so I won't say it. After another minute I rose and started to leave, but found the door through which I had entered locked. I looked around. The door on the other side of the room remained closed. I sat back down in the same single chair. I considered trying that other door, also kicking through the door into the terminal from whence I had come. But, for now, I wanted to project a frustrated traveler with nothing to hide. Then again, I had nothing to hide. Well, maybe I had a little to hide. The truth being I had quite a bit to hide.

The worst case scenario went like this: French officials and power brokers involved in Garson's weapons deals knew why I had come, and they held sufficient sway with French immigration authorities to make my visit start out prickly.

Then the door in the back wall opened. The one behind the two chairs across from me. Two men came in, one short, stocky and black followed by a tall, thin white guy. Together they gave off the image of a bowling ball closing in on the corner ten pin. They flipped open their leather badge holders: Federal Bureau of Investigation. Their manner in some ways reminded me of Charles Talmadge, only these guys had the badges that could back up their acting tough, and they likely had more grit to begin with. The FBI is supposed to be the good guys. Our guys. I'm an American, so it's okay for me to think of them as our guys. But what were they doing working in concert with French immigration to intimidate a fellow American?

The ten pin complimented me on my leather sports bag. Over time I've learned to stop telling the Tiger-bag story. Everyone, even me, eventually tires of being laughed at and called a sap. So, I gave him one of my easy smiles and said, "Thank you."

"Your business in France, Mr. Kile?" the bowling ball asked.

"The French have found my papers in order and welcomed me into their country. Why is an American law enforcement agency harassing a traveling American citizen? Beyond its jurisdiction I might add."

The ten pin answered. "We aren't harassing you, Mr. Kile. We just have a few questions. You'd like to help your government, wouldn't you?"

"I do everyday day. I obey the laws. Stop at red lights. All that stuff. In a more direct way, I pay my taxes. Very big taxes, too, I might add. I'm even back to voting, and with the choices we're been given lately voting is tough duty. And now you want more help?"

"We do have a few questions, yes," the speaking ball said.

I got up and noisily jiggled the handle on the still locked door. "I am being forcibly detained," I said, indignantly. "That is harassment, if not abduction. Unlock that door or have someone with the appropriate authority in this country arrest me. Then you may contact our embassy and tell them of my incarceration." I stood quietly next to the door, my arms folded.

"Mr. Smith," the ten pin said, "how in the world did that door get locked. If you have a key please do unlock it. Mr. Kile has every right to leave if he wishes."

"Smith? I suppose his name is Jones," I said to the Mr. Smith while he unlocked the door. Then I returned to the table and sat in the chair from which I had risen. "Now how can I help my government?"

Smith and Jones retook their seats across from me, smiled and handed me their cards: Special agents Tim Jones and Carl Smith. Darn. American phone books are filled with Smiths and Joneses, so I guess it wasn't that odd for two of them to be here with me. Still, it felt odd. I just don't know why it felt odd.

"Why are you visiting France?" Agent Smith asked.

"I am a fiction writer and I'm considering a story set partially in France. I also love French food and wine. And there are so many famous historical places here that I've never seen. Don't you think it's about time I do? Particularly if I decide to make reference to them in the story I am researching."

"Mr. Kile, let us stop wasting your time. Your government has a continuing interest in the activities of the deceased Garson Talmadge. We aren't concerned with your defense of his wife in his murder. We just request that you stop digging into his past."

"You won't have any trouble with me."

"No," said Agent Jones, with a joyless smile. "I doubt we will."

"Is it possible," I asked, "that circumstances lingering from the past may have played a role in the death of Mr. Talmadge?"

"We aren't concerned with that, Mr. Kile."

"What? Garson Talmadge died an American citizen. He was murdered. You are an American law enforcement agency. How can you sit there and say you have no interest in the solving of his murder?"

"It's a local police matter, Mr. Kile."

"Then why are you talking to me about it, Agent Smith?"

"As Agent Jones said, we have an interest in the past activities of Mr. Talmadge and we assure you there is no connection between those activities and the murder of Mr. Talmadge."

"Then who murdered Garson Talmadge?"

"We have no idea, Mr. Kile."

"Then you cannot state with certainty that there is no connection between his murder and his past activities. Can you?"

"We know all about you Matthew Kile, former tough-guy cop. Shot a man who was officially only a suspect, but who likely deserved it. Now you write, if you call that stuff writing."

"Now just a darn minute, Special Agents Smith and Jones, you can denigrate my mother, question my patriotism, even tell me I need to lose a few pounds, but don't insult my writing. Not if you want us to remain friends."

"Our apology, Mr. Kile," Agent Jones said. "Your books sell well. Americans love a great mystery."

"Speaking of that, please tell me about the past activities of Garson Talmadge to which you referred."

"I'm afraid we have no information for you, Mr. Kile."

"Well, then, Special Agent Smith, I guess my answer is the same; I'm afraid I have no information for the FBI."

"How quickly do you expect to leave France?"

"Soon."

"What does soon mean, Mr. Kile?"

"Not in the next fifteen minutes, but before later."

"How would you describe your attitude toward us, Mr. Kile?"

"Tolerant, Special Agent Jones. The FBI is interfering in the free movement and activities of an American citizen, and doing so, I might add, in a foreign country without the presence of a law enforcement official of that country."

Agent Smith repeated one of their earlier questions, "Why are you here, Mr. Kile?"

"Asked and answered, Agent Smith. Research for a possible story. Sightseeing all those wonderful things here in France that we Americans keep getting invited over to see."

"No other reasons?"

"There are a couple of people to whom I wanted to say a big heartfelt, 'how do you do.' I read somewhere that a big percentage of Europeans still think of the American West as the wild, wild west popularized in the movies. Have you heard that Special Agent Jones? I know I have."

"And who would these people be, Mr. Kile?"

"Aw shucks, now. That ain't very neighborly of y'all. Just folks who know folks I know. Just a plain old simple howdy. Sure can't be of any consequence to our big old government. Do you have anything more you wish to ask or can I mosey on up the trail?"

"So, this is your western side we're hearing from now?"

"The novel I'm working on is a western."

"A western set in France?"

"Yeah. Exciting ain't it?"

Their expressions tattled that the agents wanted me to tell them a lot more, but that they had no leverage.

They stood.

We shook hands.
I moseyed.

I found a bench outside the terminal at the de Gaulle airport and called Brad Fisher; he was behind the wheel on the way to his office. Brad agreed that the FBI being curious added credence to our theory that Talmadge had not stopped running guns ten-to-fifteen years ago or anything close to that. We also reasoned that the U.S. government might be tracing past weapons deals between French arms manufacturers and Saddam Hussein. We could see no other reason for their interest and, if they were focusing on those deals, that could well have touched a nerve that caused someone to decide Garson Talmadge was a loose thread that needed to be snipped off.

Brad would send a letter to the FBI demanding they cease interfering in his defense of an American citizen charged with the crime of murder, and requesting a copy of their file on Garson Talmadge.

Before hanging up, I asked Brad to have his paralegal look into the backgrounds of the unusual names Garson Talmadge had given his daughter and son, Sappho and Charaxus. Talmadge had named the dog he bought for his wife, Asta. That name was also unusual. Asta had been the name of the dog owned by the Dashiell Hammett character Nick Charles, the protagonist in *The Thin Man* series of books, movies and radio. It was possible Garson named his children similarly, in some private joke. It might lead nowhere, probably would lead nowhere, but we were already chasing a bunch of maybes, so why not one more.

Chapter 14

"CAPTAIN, YOU WANTED to see me?"

"Yes. Come in Sergeant Fidgery."

Chief of Detectives Richard Dickson had a smile on his face that made Fidge go tense. The term shit-eating grin captured the look.

"How's the Talmadge case progressing?" Dickson asked, without inviting Fidgery to sit down.

"I'm not sure I understand your question, sir. We have his wife, Clarice Talmadge in custody. She has been arraigned. Other than coordinating with the DA as he develops his case, I've shut it down. As you know, we have no shortage of murders."

"I understand, Sergeant, but, we both know that Brad Fisher is defending the woman. We can expect him to present alternative suspects. Let's figure out whom he might trot out for the jury's consideration. We need to be sure you've given those folks a once over."

"There is nothing clearly suggestive of any other killer."

"Imagine you're Fisher, Sergeant. Whom do you pick for the alternative shooter?"

"Fisher might toss Garson Talmadge's kids into the ring. If their stepmother is convicted, she'll likely lose her inheritance and the kids will split her portion. That could give the kids a reason to frame mommy."

"Forget that, Sergeant. Not even Fisher would think he could sell the jury on kids killing their own father, even for money. The jury will likely be parents themselves. Of course, that changes if Fisher gets some clear evidence. Could he have anything on that score?"

"Not that I know of."

"Imagine, Sergeant."

"Nothing I can imagine, sir."

"Who else?"

Fidge thought of this case as a wrap, but Chief of Detectives Dickson was toying with something. Fidge shifted his weight and spread his legs a bit farther apart. "No one else, sir. Well ... maybe the idea that old man Talmadge, who in the past dealt in the international weapons trade, had been killed by someone from that world."

"Why would they want to kill him? Your report states Talmadge had been retired for over a decade."

"You asked for guesses, then you attack them for not being solid. Guesses aren't solid, sir. That's what makes them guesses. When Talmadge retired from running guns is uncertain, as is the case with any illegal activity. His children said he stopped fifteen years ago. Talmadge's business attorney said his client had told him he stopped ten years ago. But, yes, I suspect Fisher will raise that idea, if only to cloud the jury's mind. When the jury learns Talmadge was a gun runner, they may get the impression the old man was a first-class bad guy, who simply got what he deserved. There are governments, including our own, still curious about where Saddam Hussein bought his weapons, and just which weapons he bought. That could have gotten the arms dealers with whom Talmadge did business nervous enough to eliminate him. And, assuming Talmadge had truly stopped brokering weapons, those people might see Talmadge as expendable."

"I agree, Sergeant. Fisher will raise that. No doubt. The D.A. will need to know if that theory will hold water. Look into it. Be prepared to testify you considered that theory and found it to be without merit."

"Yes. Sir."

"Any other alternative theory?"

"No. Sir."

The CD's chair squeaked as he leaned back, the shit-eating grin returning to his face. "Well I've got one for you."

"Sir?"

"What about your buddy?"

"Sir?"

"The hack writer. Your pal, Matthew Kile."

"You're kidding right?"

"Not on your life, Sergeant."

"I know you don't like Kile, but that's taking it a bit far, sir."

"Not as I see it. You need to take off your blinders, Sergeant. Look at the facts."

"Sir?"

"Kile has had an affair with Clarice Talmadge. He —"

"Now just a minute," Fidge interrupted. "Kile acknowledged having had sex with the woman. Once, before she and her husband moved in. Before Kile knew she was married. That doesn't constitute an affair."

"Let us not forget the accused and Kile both claim she was in Kile's condo when the murder occurred. In Kile's condo, I might add, well past midnight, while her husband, the victim, was supposedly asleep, not to mention the other occupants of the building. You figure their only midnight rendezvous coincidentally occurred on the night the old guy got gunned? You thinking those two had a crocheting circle? Come on, Sergeant. Open your eyes. That was about setting an alibi while both of them headed down the hall to bump off her rich old man, their mutual guilt assuring they would each hold to their shared alibi. Well, they are not about to get away with it on my watch."

"Sir, I know Matthew Kile. If he wanted, and I say 'if' he wanted this woman, he would have told her to get a divorce."

"No. No. No. With the prenup, too much money left on the table, Sergeant. The sense of urgency came with the realization that her husband was about to drop her from his will. No. They needed to do it then, that night. To wait would cost them millions."

"Kile has got money of his own. He's made a gob from his writing. He doesn't need to commit murder to gain a comfortable lifestyle."

"Your thinking is warped, Sergeant, blinded. The point is she wanted her own money. It wouldn't be the first time a hot number with a cold heart twisted a cop, an ex-cop, into doing her bidding."

"Captain Dickson, Sir, it is your right not to like Kile, but to manipulate your hatred into an accusation of murder — well, that's sick, sir."

"I'll ignore your insubordination, Sergeant. Fundamentals: Means. Motive. Opportunity. They had them all. As we both know, Kile is no stranger to violence. I plan to recommend the D.A. amend his charges to include both Clarice Talmadge and Matthew Kile."

"What do I do with this ... wild theory of yours?"

"Get after it. I want you to canvas that building. Include the super and any regular service people, housekeepers used by the various owners, like that. Let's see what those people know about this tryst. I'm betting some of the other condo owners have seen the two of them tiptoeing up and down the hall at night. They told Garson Talmadge and he decided to drop his wife from his will."

"This is a trip up fools' hill, sir. I have other cases."

"If you refuse, Sergeant, I'll reassign the Talmadge case. I can't have a detective handling a murder refusing to follow any possible trail. And this one is more than possible. It has all the elements: money, sex, greed, and a lover with a history of violence. The young wife who married the old guy for his money and learns she is being dropped from his will. It's all there, Sergeant. You only need to see it for what it is."

"I'll look into it, Captain."

"Rigorously, Sergeant."

"Rigorously, Captain Dickson."

"I will also personally be following up to talk with a few of those folks myself. So, you will be wise to make a diligent effort in that regard." Fidge clenched his teeth as Captain Dickson finished. "I want a report from you on this within three days. We'll meet at this same time. Here in my office. Good day, Sergeant Fidgery."

Chapter 15

THE TAXI THAT took me from the Charles de Gaulle Airport was driven by a Frenchman who spoke wonderful English, but had the wrong occupation. He should have been a tour guide. As he drove, he continually pointed out so many famous and interesting spots that they started to jumble together. One of the things he pointed out did get my attention, "The Center for the History of the Arab Civilization," he said. I found that interesting in that I had come, in part, to learn more about the connection between the Talmadge family and Iraq.

Many Americans who have not traveled to France probably assume every Frenchman is named Pierre. That, of course, is not true as I would find out many times over before leaving their beautiful country. Nonetheless, my driver's name was Pierre, or he simply used Pierre when driving Americans.

A few minutes and several tour-guide point-outs later, Pierre dropped me at the front of the Hotel Saint Christophe on the Rue Lacépède in the Latin Quarter of Paris, an elegant, older hotel with a welcoming air and a pleasantly bright lobby with windows overlooking the street. I paid Pierre and he gave me his cell phone number so I could reach him whenever I needed a cab.

A man sat in the lobby reading a magazine. He looked familiar. He was not someone I knew. His presence troubled me because I had seen him since my arrival in France. Without checking in, I went out to the street and walked a block to think about it. He hadn't been in the plane. I couldn't place him in the check-in-line. Then it hit me. He had some kind of connection with Agents Smith and Jones. That was it. He had been in the background when the door opened so the two agents could enter the small room where I waited. This man had walked by the open door, behind the agents, glancing in for only a moment. That's when I saw his face. He could have been an airport worker passing down a hallway at the very moment the door was opened, but more likely his passing was intentional so he could get a look and tail me after I left the airport.

I returned to the hotel, checked in, and walked to the elevator, then went back to the counter and asked to switch rooms. If the man in the lobby was a tail, he had identified my hotel in advance because he was there when I arrived. He could have persuaded the hotel's management to let him install surveillance equipment before I checked in and for the desk to assign me that particular room.

In my new room, figuring the phone would not be bugged, I immediately called Brad Fisher and brought him up to date on my suspicions.

"Aren't you being a bit paranoid?" Brad asked.

"Hey, just because I'm paranoid, doesn't mean they aren't out to get me."

Of course, I had no idea just who was out to get me, or why they were out to get me. I was simply an ant in their world and they were watching me through the glass wall of my ant farm as I went about my ant business.

After hanging up from talking with Brad I took a long walk to stretch my legs and get something to eat. The Latin Quarter had many quaint cobblestone streets that could easily allow a playful mind to imagine walking in France in an earlier century, strolling along beside Alexandre Dumas' famous quartet D'Artagnan, Aramis, Athos, and Porthos. Eventually, I chose one of the many cafes on the boulevard St-Germain-dès-Pres. During the meal I called Pierre and arranged for him to pick me up in front of my hotel at ten in the morning. I gave him the address on Rue Mercoeur and he said he knew it well. During the walk back, I thought about how I might best approach Garson's ex-wife, Chantal Talmadge.

Chapter 16

AT TEN SHARP the next morning, I walked out of the Hotel Saint Christophe to find Pierre behind the wheel of his diesel Puegeot. He got out and opened my door. I told him not to bother with that in the future; I could open my own doors. Maybe one day I wouldn't be able to, but the way I had my life planned that wouldn't be for several decades yet.

"Just be on time and get me where I need to go and I'll be a happy camper." Pierre asked me to explain what I meant by happy camper. I did. He was right. We Americans do talk funny.

The apartment house on Rue Mercoeur which we believed to be the residence of Garson's ex-wife was a masonry building of considerable age, but kept up. A sign outside indicated a vacancy. Pierre told me the sign said the available unit was a two-bedroom. My knock on Chantal's door got no answer. I checked with the building manager, who did not speak much English. I waved Pierre to come join us and he learned that Chantal had lived there with her sister, but the two women had moved. The manager wrote down the forwarding address for us. I thanked her and headed back to the car, having again proven the pessimist's creed that nothing ever goes smoothly, but then, this wasn't too big a bump so maybe the pessimists were only half right.

Pierre said something about the new address being in Latin Quarter, not far from my hotel, and drove off with me rubber necking from the back seat.

Chantal's new street was three blocks over from the Rue Monge and about eight blocks down. As we drove, Pierre pointed out Notre Dame Cathedral, and the Jardin des Plantes, France's main botanical garden. True to his claim, Pierre knew exactly where Chantal lived. He dropped me off in front. I asked him to wait twenty minutes, then, if I had not come out, he could leave and I would call his cell when I was ready to be picked up.

I pressed the small round metal button next to the door, and a pleasant chime rang inside the apartment. A few moments later, the door opened in the hand of an elderly woman in a drab, brown housecoat, unwashed gray hair, and yellowed teeth. She leaned against the door frame, her heavily-veined feet in gold slippers, one stacked on top the other. She kept one hand on the door while her tired eyes scanned my face, perhaps trying to match me up with someone in her past.

"Madame Chantal Talmadge?"

"Que?" she said with the inflection of a question.

"Madame Chantal Talmadge?" I repeated, hoping she would at least understand the name.

"I speak English"

"Are you Chantal Talmadge?"

"No."

"Is Chantal in? May I see her? I've come from America."

"Come in, sir," the woman said, with an inscrutable grin. "I'll take you to her." She uncoupled her slippers and stood back, opening the door. She led me down a short hall covered with a Persian runner, the floor creaking as if it had been laid to announce arrivals. We entered a living room with furnishings that were once up to the minute in decor. Sturdy furniture, overstuffed, and mostly covered in green velour.

She stopped facing the fireplace. "What is your name, sir?"

"Matthew Kile," I said, unsure what was going on as we were the only two people in the room.

The woman pointed to an urn on the mantle. Her hand touched it. Her voice went hoarse. "My sister, Chantal."

I had come in search of answers, and instead I found a wiseacre French woman who shared an apartment with her sister who lived in an urn. I felt like Alice must have after having fallen down the rabbit hole. I wanted to laugh. I wanted to curse even more, but I did neither. Maybe I would later.

"May I ask your name?" I said, desperate to learn something that might help.

"I am Camille Trenet. Chantal's sister. She never stopped using the name Talmadge."

"Why not?"

"Because my sister never stopped loving that worthless man. She drank herself to death, because when she drank she believed he would return and they would be happy again."

"I'm sorry for your loss."

"I'm sorry I lived long enough to go to Chantal's funeral. I would have preferred to go to the funeral of that worthless man."

"How long had you lived with Chantal?"

"We lived together all of our lives. Well, except for twenty years while I had a live-in job with an American family and Chantal lived with that worthless man. My live-in job ended about the same time as her divorce, so we picked up where we left off and moved in together again. Many women have sisters. We were best friends. Now I'm alone."

"Have you always lived in France?"

"Yes. Somehow I ended up working in the homes of American families, twenty years as a live-in with one family for whom I served as a housekeeper, the nanny and sometimes secretary. I spoke only English for all those years. Actually, despite being French, I mostly think in American and translate into French before I speak with my countrymen. I watch mostly American television, the channels I can get."

While I listened, I looked about. The place was crowded with photographs of a younger woman, who looked to be Camille, and another I surmised was Chantal, both were very lovely. The pictures featured laughter, and men, and picnics near a body of water. Another photo was of Susan and Charles when they were younger, and two more of Susan alone. And one of an American soldier, maybe twenty-five, sat on the end table next to her.

"Well, your English is very good. Is this your sister," I asked, putting my hand gently on top that picture. "May I ask you, how did your sister die?"

"I meant it literally; Chantal drank herself to death ... over that worthless man, the no-good son of a bitch."

"The worthless man you speak of, I assume you mean Garson Talmadge?"

"Who else? The dog that walks on two legs."

Camille, who had apparently gotten the stronger liver of the two sisters, ran her hands back over her head, through hair which had the look of tangled seaweed after having been pulled and snipped by gulls.

"Despite what you may have heard of French women, after that worthless man left my sister never gave herself to another man, which was very different than right after the war. The Nazis were gone and many French women had suffered at their hands. We had been too young for the Nazis and had dressed to look still younger. But that changed after the liberation. We were older by the time your boys came here, and we dressed to look still older. Your young soldiers were glorious and they always had Hershey bars and sometimes nylons. My sister and I were wild-eyed teens. We flirted with your soldiers and had a lot of laughs. If you and I were to go for a walk, I could show you many places where we satisfied sweaty American GIs. Those days were beyond description. We hoped two of them would take us back to America, but the magic ended. They left. We remained." She laughed openly, her eyes searching back for the memories. "In France, girls are considered women at a younger age than in America, at least in those days, probably still. My memory only remembers the fun of those years, not the cruelty. There was so much destruction. Chantal and I were gorgeous in those days. Love was always in the air and chocolate flowed like water."

After laughing, hard enough to cause her to cough and then swallow, she added, "These silly modern women think they invented not wearing panties so their ass will wiggle more. Ha." Then she got up and turned around slowly in her house dress. "You like? My tits are bigger now. Then again, so is everything else." It had not been so much an invitation as an expression of whom she had been and whom she had become. After pursing her lips, she laughed, a sadder laugh than before.

"Do you know that Garson Talmadge is dead?" I asked, still standing, facing the urn.

Camille turned to me, her face blank. No words. She just stared.

"He was murdered," I said.

"I don't know whether to laugh or cheer," she finally said. "I will likely do both later when I am alone." Camille touched my arm and nodded toward her couch. I sat down. She sat across from me in a swivel rocker. The flower-pattern fabric on the arm of the chair above the wooden tip excreted its soiled white stuffing.

"Why are you here?" She asked. "I did not kill him. Although, given the chance ..." Her stare continued while I imagined her mind reviewing the ways she had fantasized murdering him if she had ever had the chance. She now knew that chance would never come. "Who beat me to it?"

"That's what brought me over. His wife, Clarice, has been charged with his murder. I'm investigating for the attorney who is defending her. We believe Clarice is innocent."

"Whether she is guilty or innocent is irrelevant. The man deserved to die so, even if she did murder him, I will help if I can. But I don't see how I ..." Camille apparently had a habit of leaving things she spoke of unfinished, maybe simply crowded out by a memory. If her apartment expressed anything, it said Camille Trenet lives in her past.

"I have come to learn all that I can about Garson when he lived in France, about his son and daughter and his weapons deals. What do you know about his selling French weapons to Saddam Hussein, or anyone else?"

"I do wish to help. Hurray for the wonderful woman who killed that worthless man."

"Alleged," I said in a correcting tone.

"Huh," she mumbled. "Oh, yes, American lawyer talk I hear it on television. Let me get us something to drink, and then I'll answer your questions. This may be a long conversation. Things I have never told anyone. Chantal had sworn me to secrecy, but she is dead now. And that worthless man is dead. The time has come to drag the ugliness out of the darkness."

By now, Pierre would have likely driven away. I would call his cell when I finished visiting with Garson's ex-wife's sister.

Camille opened the door on a cabinet in the lower part of the end table next to her chair and brought out a half full bottle of Seagram's Seven Crown, her chubby hand strangling its neck. "American whiskey, my sister started drinking this stuff with that worthless man." She reached in again and brought out two glasses, her fingers inside as she lifted them to the bigger table that centered the space between us. "Is this to your liking?" she asked.

"Just fine," I said, and then smiled. "I am, in fact, an Irish whiskey man. Once you have sipped Tullamore Dew you are spoiled for all spirits made by mortals. Although, in fairness there are many other fine Irish, Scottish, Canadian and American whiskeys, like this one. Thank you."

Camille served her Seagram's Seven already warm in portions for gulping. I confess Seagram makes a fine product, but my ancestors would label me traitor if I did less than my duty to carry the family tradition through my generation, and pass it along to those who follow. I proudly say that both my daughters have already accepted their responsibilities in this regard. Hopefully, my ancestors will forgive my transgressions and remain calm in their final resting places.

I had likely shared with her more about Irish whiskey than she ever cared to know, but she came across as lonely and enjoying the idea of someone, a man, to drink with. I needed her comfortable and relaxed and willing to talk. She was no longer anything to look at, and half soused, but I liked her and her bunny slippers were cute.

I picked up my glass. "You were about to tell me about Garson's weapons deals with Iraq."

"It is true, according to Chantal, who never lied to me. That worthless man sold nearly exclusively to Saddam Hussein, guns, bullets, even tanks and those big trucks they use to transport soldiers. Chemicals, too, Chantal said. My sister also said that worthless man gambled like a crazy man or he would have had far more than he did when he retired. I remember her telling me of one spree in Monte Carlo where he lost ten million dollars in one week. And there were other times, many times, when he lost huge amounts."

"It has been said that Garson stopped selling weapons about ten or fifteen years ago. Is this true?"

"That I don't know. Chantal had no more contact with that worthless man once he divorced her and moved to America. Her divorce deal included him providing money for as long as either of us lived."

"How did they breakup?"

"Now that's an odd story." Camille leaned forward and again reached into the cabinet, this time to bring out a large bar of chocolate. "One day," she said, "when that worthless man was driving Chantal over to my place, he pulled into a store to buy some cigarettes. He never came out. After waiting a long while, Chantal went in, but he was not in the store. My sister worried that he had been killed. I hoped he had. He always made my sister swear that she would never go to the police about him no matter what. She had promised, and so she kept her promise. She continued to wait and pray for his return. The next year, she learned he was still alive when his attorney contacted her about his wanting a divorce."

Camille used her hands to break up the chocolate bar while it was still inside its package. She tore open the wrapper, took out a large jagged piece and pushed the rest toward the center of the table as an offering. We had bonded.

"What about Susan and Charles, were they still with your sister?"

"Oh, no. The kids were grown, in their twenties. They had their own places before the divorce. My sister continued to see them. At least she did until he convinced them both to go to America with him. Susan had always wanted to live in America. Charles didn't really care, but he went when his sister did. They worked for that worthless man so they also went to keep their jobs."

"But Garson was supposedly no longer doing weapons deals. What kind of work were the children doing at that point?"

"Search me," she said with a shrug. "After waiting a year without contacting my sister, that worthless man wanted the divorce and fast, so he went along with whatever my sister wanted in return. She got enough money on the front end to allow her to buy our last condo. She left it to me. I sold it a while back and bought this smaller one. When there was only me I didn't need all the space. He also sends money for food and utilities and whatever. I make do with that and what little I get elsewhere. Now that he is dead, I don't know what will happen to me. But I am still happy he is dead. I hope someday to spit on his grave."

"His will," I explained, "includes a provision for continuing your assistance even if he were to die before Chantal or you. Susan is the personal representative named in his will. I expect she will see that whatever is necessary for you continues."

"Thank you for telling me, sir." She raised her glass in my direction, took a drink, and then refilled hers and topped off mine. "I hate taking that worthless man's money. But it allows me to live. I remain alive to curse his remains."

"His children, where did he come up with the names Sappho and Charaxus?"

"Yes," she said, stretching the word as if it were a pull on soft taffy. "Sappho was always a bright girl with a good heart and a warm smile. Charaxus is a bore. Nasty. I never liked him."

"You'll be pleased to know that Susan, the name now used by Sappho, is still a bright, good-hearted woman with a wonderful smile."

"And the boy?"

"He is still a bore. Nasty. I don't like him either. But I was asking about the story behind Garson's choice of names for the children."

Camille nodded slightly, and then licked chocolate residue from her fingers. She leaned across the space between us, her house dress creeping up far enough to expose nylons rolled down to just below her knee. We clinked glasses and shared agreeable smiles. "I have no idea," she said. "They were odd names, but why I don't know."

"Was Chantal the mother?"

"No. No." She took another jagged chunk of chocolate. "Chantal could not have children. That is why my sister went along with the arrangement."

"The arrangement?" I asked. "It is my understanding that Garson Talmadge had an affair with an Iraqi woman who gave birth to his children. That is what the children believe as well, as least I think they do."

"That worthless man never told the truth about anything in his life. Not only was my sister not the mother of those children, that man was not the children's father."

My thoughts went into overdrive. Could Brad Fisher use this woman's statement to get a court order for DNA testing to prove Garson was not the father? Might a jury more easily believe that children might kill their father when their father is not their father? And that's a lot of fathers in one sentence, but you get the idea.

"Camille, do Susan and Charles know that Garson is not their father?"

"I do not think so. Or maybe I should have said they did not when they left here for America. Now," she shrugged, "who knows."

"Garson Talmadge never impressed me as a man who would raise another man's children. Why would he do it?"

Camille drained her glass and reached for the bottle with a practiced knowledge of its whereabouts. "For the only reason that worthless man did anything, money."

"Who was the father?"

She refilled her drink far enough for it to show in the glass above her fist. "Chantal never knew the father's name. He was some big shot in the weapons business." After another finger lick, she picked up the last piece of broken chocolate.

I didn't give a rip about Camille's chocolate fetish. I needed to get the rest of the story before she drank too much more. Although, her speech remained amazingly clear despite what she had drank already. I fought down my impatience and casually asked, "Tell me what your sister told you about the Frenchman who fathered Susan and Charles."

She emptied the bottle, refilling her glass and what little would fit into mine. "All this talk keeps me thirsty." Then she told more of her story, well, her sister's story. "It happened on one of that worthless man's visits to Iraq. The Frenchman went along and while they were there, the government provided them with women, Shiite women. Saddam was Sunni.

The woman the Frenchman had been with became pregnant and died giving birth to twins. With the mother dead the story was that Saddam planned to have the children killed. To his credit, when the Frenchman learned of it he contacted Hussein and said he did not want the children put to death. But he could not bring them home to his French family. So, that worthless man brought the children back to Paris for my sister to raise."

"How do you know this?"

"Chantal had always wanted children, but she could not have them. At first, he told her the children were his hoping that way she would be more likely to accept them. Chantal forgave him and went along. Later, he admitted the truth about the Frenchman being the father. He also told her that the Frenchman had not wanted them killed. The Frenchman gave the worthless man a great deal of money to raise them as his children and brought him in on a bunch more weapons deals. No. They are not his children. Of that there is no doubt."

"Camille, isn't it possible that what Garson first told your sister was the truth, that he was the father?"

She reached into the cabinet and brought out a second bottle. "My last one," she said while breaking the seal. "I think they're making these bottles smaller nowadays." When she had loosened the cap, she said, "That could not be true."

"Why?"

"Chantal always said she could not have children, but it was that man who could not. They had both been checked by the doctor before he went to Iraq with the Frenchman. The results came in while he was gone. Chantal went to the doctor alone where she learned she was fertile, but that worthless man was sterile. She had known all along that her worthless man was lying about fathering those two. Chantal always said it was she who could not conceive because she believed that should he know the truth, he would feel less virile. It was many years later that he finally told Chantal the truth about someone else being the father and paying him to raise the children. My sister would do anything for that worthless man. He was the only thing we did not agree about."

I asked the next question after reminding myself to keep the tone conversational. "Do you know the identity of the Frenchman who was the father?"

"Chantal never knew so she could never tell me. That worthless man kept the Frenchman's secret all those years, and now it has apparently died with him. After Chantal died I tried to find out who he was, but there is no records kept on these illegal deals."

After calling Pierre, I talked further with Camille Trenet, but she knew nothing more. Twenty-five minutes later, Pierre dropped me off in front of my hotel. On the way he had pointed out the Sorbonne, a place known for the arts and humanities, but my attention was not on the sights of Paris.

Chapter 17

THE MAN I had first seen through the open door passing behind Agents Smith and Jones at the airport, and later saw again in my hotel lobby, had left me uncertain about the phone in my hotel room. I had switched rooms, but by now he could have moved his surveillance equipment to my new room. I wandered outside, found a bench and called Brad Fisher on my cell phone.

Brad's amazement over what I had encountered since arriving in France matched my own. This had become something more than the quick, quiet visit to France we had anticipated. If Garson Talmadge had stopped moving weapons for profit nearly fifteen years ago, what had happened to stir up the interest of the FBI? We didn't know, but we needed to.

We discussed having a French lawyer take Camille's sworn statement so Brad could use it to support an attempt to obtain a court order for Susan's and her brother's DNA, if they refused to do so voluntarily. Conversely, if they knew they were not his children they might fight it all the way. At least that was our reasoning.

Brad insisted I get Camille to sign an affidavit before I left, and to agree she would come to Long Beach to testify. In return, we would offer her all expenses paid, a case of chocolate bars, and the opportunity to spit on Garson's grave. I figured the last item would seal the deal.

After Brad hung up, I returned to my hotel and took a hot shower. The chocolate that had been in my stomach the past several hours pickling in Seagram's Seven had begun the second French Revolution. I wished I was an astronaut in outer space where the absence of gravity prevented the separation of liquids and gas necessary for the production of belches and farts.

After showering, I went back onto the streets desperate for something to eat, found a café and ordered a Salade Nicoise, a Croque Monsieur, which the menu described as a baked ham sandwich with garlic cream sauce and Swiss cheese, and topped it all off with Strawberries Romanoff.

While sipping coffee, my mind reworked what I had learned and my discussion with Brad Fisher. The chances of directing the jury to the theory that Susan and Charles might have killed Garson Talmadge had improved with the prospect they were not his children, at least according to Chantal's sister, Camille. Had Susan and Charles learned that Garson was not their father they would likely have confronted Garson to learn the identity of their real father. My reasoning said that he refused to tell them. Under this scenario Charles and Susan may have killed him; if so, I hoped it had only been Charles.

We also had to face the possibility that Charles was telling the truth, that Garson had called him to say he was dropping Clarice from his will. That Garson had told Clarice of his plan during one of their arguments, so Clarice killed him before he could change his will. Then she could claim she knew nothing regarding his desire to change his will in any manner, and no motive to kill him.

The scenario I favored, and which had the most external support remained that people in France and the Middle East who had been the sellers and buyers of the weapons Garson had brokered had killed him in the hope of stonewalling the authorities who were digging into those transactions. Maybe this all started because of documents found in Iraq. Why else would the FBI corner me at the airport? Why else would they want to know what brought me to France? Even more basic: why else would the FBI even be aware I was in France? This scenario had legs, but walking this pile of conjecture into court would be an entirely different matter.

All this was what I loved and hated about investigative work, the endless combination of twists and turns that denied sleep and the freedom to think about much of anything else.

After finishing the Strawberries Romanoff, I walked back to the Hotel Saint Christophe. Having had the wrong address for Chantal had been a minor irritant. The kind of inconvenience one expects in an investigation. Chantal being dead, however, was a major wrinkle. Her sister had been helpful, but it made everything she knew secondhand. Camille's testimony, with respect to things her sister told her, might even be challenged as inadmissible hearsay because Chantal would not be in the court to be cross examined. But that would be Brad Fisher's battle to fight another day. My job remained to bring Brad information related to Garson Talmadge.

I didn't like the attempt by the FBI to intimidate me off the case, or at least out of France. But all things considered, the trip was proving to be worth the effort. On the whole, things had gone well. At least they had until someone fired a shot at me.

Anyone who has survived a tour of duty in a war zone or been a cop on the street would instinctively recognize the sound and know what to do. The bullet whizzed by and struck the wall of a shop where I had just paused to look at their window display. I dove into the sidewalk, a literal effort denied by aged cobblestones. I rolled sideways tightening myself to a parked car, my right foot dropping into gutter water.

The shot had come from across the street. The sound reported the bullet struck low on the shop wall. That meant the shooter had fired from higher up. A window? The rooftop? If the shooter had been lower, the shot would have been blocked by one of the parked cars, not the building wall.

I stayed where I was, well, I did other than lifting my foot back out of the dank water. The next minute passed with no more shots coming, then two minutes. I held my position and listened for the violent sound of a speeding car arriving or departing the scene. But I heard nothing. Not even the commotion of feet running across the cobblestones. Nothing that said they were closing in for the kill.

I stayed low and scooted to the end of the car. There were no pedestrians within a block on my side of the street. Across, on the other side, one couple had stopped and looked around, then, apparently unable to identify the noise, they walked on. From my crouch I glanced at the rooftop. Then studied the windows of the building one by one, from left to right, floor by floor, but saw nothing that seemed to relate to the shot that had been fired. After five minutes, I rose slowly and continued back toward my hotel.

By the end of the next block, I had decided the objective of the shooter was not to murder me. There had been no additional shots. No one had moved in to finish me off. This had been a warning. A message: Yankee, go home! Stop asking questions and leave France.

I wasn't going to stop asking questions, so I could only hope the warning shot was as far as they were prepared to take it. Of course, that might change if I continued to crowd the truth which is exactly what I planned to do.

I detoured into a bar about a block from the hotel and ordered a straight shot of whiskey. They didn't have Irish so I settled for Scotch, threw it back without bothering to sit down, dropped a five, U.S., on the bar and walked out. I would not report the shooting, doing that would not tell me who had fired the shot. A formal report would be a distraction, resulting in the French police pressing me to learn why I had come to France. Unlike with the FBI, given a shooting within their jurisdiction, this would be a legitimate question I would likely need to answer. I didn't wish to do that.

My adrenaline was still surging when I got back to the hotel so I walked past the elevator and took the stairs. When I entered my room, I knew my night was not over.

Chapter 18

TWO MEN, AS it turned out police detectives, were waiting inside my hotel room. Both wore their big bad wolf huffing-and-puffing looks. I replied with my best you-can't-blow-my-house-down stare, hoping at the same time that mine would be the brick house and not the one made of straw. After another minute of sniffing each other, the smaller man introduced himself.

"I am Sergeant Maurice Reynie. Please call me Maurice." He also replaced his big-bad-wolf look with a welcome-to-France smile. He was a man in his mid sixties, his fleshy jowls tugging the ends of his mouth into a reverse happy face. Still, his smile was pleasant enough.

The second officer, a bigger man, remained silent and Maurice did not introduce him. Perhaps the bigger fellow had never been taught the welcome-to-France smile. Perhaps he had no interest in learning it. Despite his being the younger of the two, I pegged him as the senior officer who wanted to size me up without having to engage in conversation.

"So you are with the Paris police?" I asked.

"Not quite," Maurice said. "The Prefecture of Police is the national police force, but we are charged with providing policing services within Paris and some surrounding areas."

"So, what is it that I, a mere tourist, can do to aid the French National Police?"

"It has come to our attention you are here to look into, shall I say, the background of a former French citizen, Garson Talmadge, now an American citizen," Maurice said. "Why do you have that interest, Mr. Kile?"

"Now wait just a minute. If I am to call you Maurice, you should call me Matt. And, please do sit down Maurice and your quiet friend of course. I'm sorry I have nothing to offer you. We could order something in, if you'd like?"

"No thank you, Monsieur. That won't be necessary. All right, Matt, please answer my question."

"If, as you contend, my visit involves this Mr. Talmadge, I would be here looking into the background of an American citizen. Why does that involve the French National Police?"

"As you are undoubtedly aware," the French detective said, "it has been claimed in certain circles that Garson Talmadge had, many years ago, functioned as a broker of illegal weapons. While that was never proven, the reputation exists. Naturally, that raises the curiosity of my country."

I furrowed my brow before replying. "The raising of that curiosity suggests those deals did occur and that French defense industrialists and politicians were involved."

"Why so? My former countryman could have sold weapons produced anywhere, not just in France."

"You have stated this Mr. Talmadge is no longer a citizen, and no longer a resident of France. If French merchants and politicians were not involved, you would not be here."

"He was a citizen of France while allegedly doing these weapons deals and, as the French National Police, we take such possibilities very seriously."

"A fact confirmed by the long list of arrests you have made over the years of people in your government and industry who are engaged in such naughty behavior."

"That was a low blow, as you Americans say."

I laughed. "Yeah, I guess it was. Not that it makes it any less valid."

"How much longer do you plan to grace us with your company, Mr. Kile?" The heretofore silent second officer asked, still offering neither his name nor rank.

"A day or two, I would imagine, although, one can never be certain. France is such a romantic and welcoming country. May I add that my primary reason for visiting your lovely country is research regarding a fiction story I am considering writing."

The second officer spoke again, still without smiling. "Ah, yes, the American novelist, I thought your name sounded familiar. Of course, please enjoy our national hospitality. And should we be able to be of any help with regard to your fiction research, please do contact Maurice. Now, as for Garson Talmadge, the past is best left alone, Mr. Kile."

"An interesting point, but one which carried to its full conclusion would prevent all investigations for, by their very nature, all crimes occurred in the past."

The senior intimidator having taken the lead, kept it. "Monsieur Kile, I will ask you again. Why are you investigating Garson Talmadge?"

"My inquiries in France, whether they regard Mr. Talmadge or not, are being done in the service of an American attorney at law, Bradford Fisher, Long Beach, California. He would be the appropriate person for you to ask your question."

"It is late," the senior man said. "Let us leave you to rest so that you can have a full day tomorrow. That way, perhaps you can wrap up your visit in one more day, rather than two."

"I thought the French tourist industry wanted visits from Americans to be longer, not shorter."

The unnamed man grunted before saying, "We are not with the tourist bureau." He then looked at Maurice and nodded. They stood.

"Good night, Matt," Maurice said.

"Good night, Maurice. Perhaps next time you could call first rather than taking the liberty of simply entering my room."

"Enjoy your day tomorrow," the senior detective said. "Paris is a wonderful city in so many ways. We are primarily concerned with your safety, so we certainly hope you do not have any more incidents like the one that troubled you during your walk back to your room tonight."

The inference had been clear. They knew about the shot across my bow. I doubted they had done it because they might not have had sufficient time to get into my room before I got back to the hotel. They also knew I knew they knew. Police work is such fun. Actually, I sort of liked their style of intimidation, waiting in someone's room when you're not expected, and preceding your questions with a warning shot. Maybe I would have been a more successful cop in France than I had been in America where the criminal process has gradually, but persistently tilted to the favor of the suspect.

"Thank you both for your concern. I'll count on your protective oversight during the remainder of my stay. Good night, gentlemen."

After closing the door, I walked out onto the small balcony through, as you would expect, a French door. The evening profile of Paris stood before me, crowned with flickering lights, night noises, and the wonderfully mixed fragrances of French cuisine.

A few things had become clear. The French Police could not have known about the warning shot without having been culpable on some level. I also knew their interest in my visit had nothing to do with the guilt or innocence of Clarice Talmadge.

Somewhere in France was a powerful politician or industrialist whom I was making more nervous than he was making me. Hopefully, that imbalance would remain in my favor.

Chapter 19

PIERRE HAD A cousin with a warehouse a few miles out of our way where I could pick up a case of Seagram's Seven Crown. It would be my thanks, well, bribe for Camille Trenet. On impulse I had Pierre stop once more so I could get a case of chocolate bars. How could any woman resist a man who came calling with whiskey and chocolate?

Camille smiled when she saw me at her door. Her smile widened when she saw the case I had under my arm. From there she went giddy upon seeing the case of chocolate bars I held in my other hand, her gladness more a product of her loneliness and unique dietary passions than my magnanimity.

She immediately opened the case of whiskey and placed all twelve bottles inside the cabinet in the base of her living room table, taking care to turn each label to the front. She then opened the box of large chocolate bars and slid them one by one into the drawer above the bottle cabinet. Each bar turned so that the label faced up and read from left to right. We all have our rituals, and this was one of hers. I decided right then I would give this colorful quirk to some character in one of my novels.

Camille unhesitatingly agreed to give a sworn statement through a Paris attorney, come to America to testify, or both, all expenses paid of course. A belly laugh followed my saying if she came to America I would also take her to spit on Garson Talmadge's grave.

"Whom did you tell about my visiting with you yesterday?"

"No one," she said immediately.

I believed her. Still, when Maurice and the intimidator visited my room last night, they knew why I had come to Paris. So had the FBI agents Smith and Jones with whom I visited at the airport. That meant either Clarice, Susan, Brad Fisher or I had told someone, who told someone, who told someone, well, you get the idea. No one else had known. I quickly eliminated Brad and myself, leaving Clarice and Susan, and maybe her brother Charles. If it had been Charles then Susan would have been the tattletale and Charles the first someone she had told and he had told someone else. Someone within the circle of the case was talking to the authorities, likely to the American FBI, who then passed it on to the Paris police. At this point, the why was up for grabs.

Camille understood, at least in a general sense, why her sworn statement and/or testimony would be needed, given that her sister, Garson's former wife, was dead.

Then she surprised me, again. "What about my sister's diary? Would that help?"

"Did Chantal keep a diary?" My pulse quickened. "Do you have it?"

"Who else?" Camille said. "However, I'll need it back. It's the only thing I have that is in my sister's own words." She added that she would be willing to testify that the writings in the diary were her sister's. She also had various documents that her sister had signed which could be used by a graphologist to verify the diary had been written by Chantal.

She went on to explain her sister had kept the diary faithfully during her marriage to Garson and the anguish she had lived through waiting for the day Garson would return, a day that never came.

"And you were familiar with the diary during those years?"

"Sure I was. During their married years Chantal kept the diary in French, but after he left and went to America my sister convinced herself he would return for her. The first year after he left, Chantal insisted every day I help her with her English so she would be ready when that worthless man returned from America. Chantal had always spoken quite a bit of English, ever since the war, but she couldn't write a lick of it. We agreed to only speak English in the house and I taught her how to write it. She practiced tirelessly. When she got good enough she bought a new diary and rewrote her old diary in English, that's the one I gave you."

"What happened to the one in French?"

"She threw it out after she had rewritten it in English. It was a big accomplishment and Chantal was very proud of having done it."

That Camille was pleased by Garson's death was obvious each time it came up. It seemed equally clear that she would want to help Clarice whether or not she had killed "that worthless man," as Camille had consistently referred to Garson Talmadge. I would alert Brad Fisher that he had a witness who might be induced to express her hatred for Garson and desire to reward, not punish, his killer. Such an admission by Camille during her testimony would damage her credibility as a witness.

Camille had not yet cleaned up. We agreed she would do so while I called the attorney, Brad Fisher, in California. Brad was in a conference, but I convinced his secretary that she should get him, now. After I told him about the diary, he wanted a sworn affidavit signed by Camille that began: *that certain diary first showing – whatever date it first shows – and titled on the inside page as The Diary of Chantal Talmadge*, was Camille's sister's diary, in Chantal's handwriting. And that Camille Trenet had observed her sister write in it regularly over the many years they had lived together. And that Camille Trenet remembers her sister, Chantal, freely discussing its contents and the events described therein.

Before Camille came out, I had lined up an attorney not far from her home and, after offering double his normal fee, made an appointment for forty-five minutes later. Pierre, whom I had retained for the day, drove us. The meeting took nearly two hours. I paid the attorney and took Camille back home.

At four-thirty that afternoon, Pierre drove me back to the hotel, agreeing to pick me up at six the next morning and take me directly to the Charles de Gaulle airport. Pierre had been on time and fully cooperative, so I offered to again hire him for all of tomorrow at the daily rate even though I would not need him after about nine in the morning. I would be his last fare tonight and his first fare tomorrow morning. We agreed I would pay him for today and tomorrow when he dropped me at the airport.

Before getting out of Pierre's cab in front of my hotel, my mind somehow found an idea. I'm not sure why, instinct perhaps, but I decided that on some level it felt smart.

I went up to my room, dropped my portfolio on the bed and went back out onto the boulevard. After walking four blocks, I stopped for a bite in the same café on the Boulevard St-Germain dès-Pres where I had eaten the prior night. I considered trying a new spot, but it would be my last night in Paris and I remembered several things on their menu that looked interesting.

An hour later, not wanting to get lost, I walked the same path I had taken the night before. As I neared where the shot had been fired at me, I kept an eye on the building from which I thought the shot had come. I passed the area without incident, took a deep breath, and returned to the Hotel Saint Christophe.

The first thing I saw after flipping on the recessed entry light inside my room was my portfolio which remained on the bed where I had left it, but it had been moved. I had left it lying lengthwise like a person would sleep on the bed. It now lay sideways, across the bed. The bottom dresser drawer, the one that stuck each time if not jiggled while partway closed, was crooked. My suitcase was in the position I had left it, but the zipper was not. I always brought the two zippers together precisely in the middle of the left side of the case, an easy way to determine if someone had gone through it during my absence.

The next thing I knew, I dropped to my knees, stunned, my mind feeling as gooey and wet as a well digger's handkerchief.

I had not been knocked out, but the blow to the back of my neck had been strong enough to leave my vision hunting for a way through a sky of dancing light spots. Maybe I wanted to find the identity of who had hit me, or maybe why whoever had hit me, had hit me, or maybe more basic than that, I just wanted to be sure who I was.

It had been the kind of blow that made you forget everything beyond bladder control, but a moment later it all came rushing back. I have been similarly close to knocked out on several other occasions. I could not recall a single one being pleasant. Tonight was no exception.

I got my arms under me and tried to rise, but fell back. Right then, I could have crawled under the belly of a duck, but standing up was a no-can-do. After a major effort, I got one knee pulled under me. Then a wire encircled my neck, and a large foot pressed hard against the small of my back. For the third time, I went back to the floor face down, a short distance from where I had a moment before hovered on my elbows.

The foot moved up between my shoulder blades.

The wire tightened.

The strong, unloving hands of a different man patted my pockets and my sides, then the cuffs of my pants near the ankles, and finally the contour of my back. They had found no gun because I was not carrying a gun.

I had at least two visitors. The one with the wire kept it taut enough that I could feel some of my blood making good its escape across my neck. Whoever these mugs were, they did not come for a quick kill. If they had, I would already be dead. Small as it was, that element was in my favor. It was about all I had.

The one with the frisky hands stepped to one side. I heard him take out a handgun and bring one into the chamber. The man with the wire loosened it, slipped it back off my head, and took his foot from my back. From where I remained, I could peripherally see a pair of men's shoes standing to each side, six feet or so from where my lips were kissing the carpet. The man to my left had the bigger feet. Although at this point I was only assuming they were men. They could have been women with the strength and feet of men.

The one with the gun barked out instructions. The ones with the guns always get to do that.

"Get your back against the footboard," he said, punctuating his command by striking the side of my thigh with the barrel of his gun. "Legs out front, feet spread, back of the knees touching the carpet."

Under the circumstances, I did exactly as I was told, something which I have always found distasteful. I make exceptions when the teller has a gun pointed at most any part of my body. This time the gun pointed at my groin.

"Don't move," said the man on the other side of me. "If you do, you won't move again until someone else picks you up, and you won't know it when they do."

I looked from one to the other. They both wore stocking masks with rough cutouts for their eyes and mouth. They had to be hot in those things. I liked that thought; I liked it a lot. I also liked the fact that I wasn't already dead. I liked that a lot, too. They wanted to talk. Maybe kill me afterwards, but talk first. So I had some time, to do what I didn't know, but right now additional time was more rewarding than hitting the lottery.

"Thanks for stopping by," I said. "I've never been made to feel so welcome in a new land. Are you fellows with the Paris tourist bureau? I can't seem to find anyone who is."

"Always the smart mouth, aren't ya." The larger man snapped his head toward the one who had spoken. He knew what I knew. The talker had screwed up. Another piece of the puzzle had dropped in place, a small piece. If they were familiar with my mouth, they likely knew my name.

This wasn't a random burglary surprised by a returning hotel guest. His voice had reminded me of the quiet French detective who had visited me along with the more talkative detective Maurice Reynie, but this guy spoke English without a French accent. Maybe these two weren't Twiddle Dee and Twiddle Dum from the Prefecture of Police. Or maybe they were and this guy had developed the skill to vary his accent. This one was in charge and the ones in charge get to be in charge because they have more skills than the ones who are not in charge. At least that's the way the system is supposed to work, but we all know folks who have advanced beyond their skills to remain in one position and clog things up the folks below them in the chain of command. In any event, his comment about my smart mouth, the *always* part, while likely true, confirmed that at least one of tonight's visitors had talked with me before. My learning this was one of the benefits of having a unique personality or, as he had put it, a smart mouth. It also had the drawback of increasing the possibility that they would end this talk with a bullet in my head.

It's been said that when one is facing death that their life flashes before them. If so, those thoughts would need to be compressed like a computer zip file. I mean, no killer is going to sit around while his prey reviews his life. With this idea in mind I thought about my ex-wife and her encouraging me to improve the behavior of my mouth. I always promised, but it was time to confess I never worked at it very hard. My poor effort on that score played a role in our divorce, although probably not a big role. There were other bigger issues, but that's another story. Still, seeing I might soon be facing my maker, I should admit that at least half, if not more, of those issues, well, okay more than half, much more than half, were my issues, not hers. But she had some of her own as well, which, to her credit, she admitted. Well, sort of admitted. Women will say things like I realize that some of this may be my fault. You notice the words don't say *is* my fault, but *may be* my fault. In my ex's case, she said, "It's possible; I may not have sufficiently catered to your desire to be visually enticed." Again, as you undoubtedly noticed, she did not say, "I *did not*," but "I *may not have*." I always felt admissions without an apology tagging along with a commitment to try and change lacked any promise that things would really get better. And they never did; she probably felt the same way. As for apologies, I apologize for boring you with this review of my failed marriage, but I may not get another chance and I needed to get it off my chest. Then again, this is something I should discuss with my therapist, as soon as I get one, and not all of you, at least not right now, my visitors were waiting. In my head, all this took less time than it took you to read it.

"Where is it, Kile?" The bigger man asked probably after deciding he had given me enough time to mentally reminisce about my ex-wife and our respective contributions to our divorce.

"Where is what?" I asked in reply, doubting that they knew. They were fishing to see if I had gotten anything from Camille.

"Don't fool with us. Where is it?"

"I don't know what —" Then the shot rang out. Well, spit out. The gun was wearing a noise suppressor. The bullet hit the wooden post of the double bed a foot from my right ear. Wood shavings slapped my cheek. I flinched.

"Your last warning, Kile. Give it up."

"Hey, guys. Whoever you are, you've already rifled my luggage and searched my person. I'm clueless. I have only what I came with. I haven't even bought any mementoes to take home to my loved ones."

The next shot tore out another chunk, this time from the opposite foot post a bit farther from my head. That part was good. This shot had been fired by the man on the other side of me.

"I hope you two are hitting the foot posts because you're good shots and not because you're bad shots. Bottom line, guys, you can search me and my things as long as you want. Take anything you find that appeals to you. Hell, take all of it and sort it out later. I don't know what you want. I don't know what to do here."

"Tell us about your visit today with Camille Trenet."

"What? Oh my God. That. Sure. I was looking for a woman named Chantal Talmadge. Turns out the woman has been dead for years; I don't know exactly how long. Camille Trenet is her sister. For me, the visit was a dead-end, although, right at the moment I don't like using the word *dead* in any context."

"You were there yesterday as well. Why two days?"

"Can I move my hand? The blood on my neck is feeling ... icky."

"Slowly."

"Okay," I said after wiping. "Yesterday, I went looking for Chantal and found her sister, Camille. We visited for a few hours, a big waste."

"What was your interest in Chantal Talmadge?" The guy to my right was doing most of the questioning. On that question, his accent seemed a bit more pronounced.

"An attorney in Long Beach, California, is defending a woman named Clarice Talmadge for the murder of her husband, Garson Talmadge who got shot dead last week. Chantal is a former wife of Garson Talmadge. The attorney wanted to check all the angles. He sent me to see if Chantal could tell us anything that might help defend Clarice."

"Exactly what did this attorney want to know?"

"Anything. This was a fishing expedition. We wondered if Garson had stayed in touch with Chantal, maybe written to her about his relations with Clarice. Anything at all that might argue against Clarice having killed Garson. If we had known Chantal was dead I wouldn't even be here."

"What else?"

"He was curious about the Talmadge children. That's pretty much it. Like I say, the attorney's fishing. I think he's daffy, but what the hell I get expenses and my daily rate to visit France."

"Why does this attorney want to know about the kids? Before you answer, get up slowly and move onto the bed with your back against the headboard. Put your feet back like they are now. Hands crossed in front of you. Do it."

I moved onto the bed.

"The kids?" He repeated.

"Nothing. Everything. Anything. I'm guessing here, but attorneys in murder cases often want to find other possible suspects. If they can get the jury to wonder if someone else killed the guy, then the jury may develop reasonable doubt. That's a big thing, reasonable doubt, in American murder trials. There weren't a lot of folks to pick from to promote the alternative killer theory. The kids would get a good amount of money from their papa's will. Might they have killed him to get to it sooner? Maybe Chantal, the ex-wife came over to get revenge and she killed him. She would make an excellent alternative killer, but that didn't work, her being dead and all. Like I said, I'm guessing here, the frigging attorney only tells me so much, but it makes no sense to me. Kids don't go around killing their fathers. It's a nutty idea, but hey, like I said, I got an expense paid trip to Paris. Why should I complain? Right?"

"Roll over on your face, feet and arms apart. Spread eagle."

I did.

"Why did you go back today?"

I felt the bed move. Then I heard a digging sound, more like gouging than digging. One of my guests was retrieving the bullets from the foot posts.

"That was nothing. Camille likes to drink. When I was there, she promised she would contact me if she thought of anything. Standard investigation stuff, you know, if you think of anything further please get in touch with me. My flight out wasn't until tomorrow morning so I took her a case of her favorite whiskey. That woman can really put it away. I figured a token gesture might make her feel good toward me so she would call on the off chance she did think of anything. Hey, it's fun spending an expense account. I would've bought you guys something if I had known you'd be stopping by."

"Where did you take her?" The voice came from the other side, the side from where I felt the bed moving.

"Oh that? She got to drinking and talking about her sister dying without a will. Said she had to get her own will drawn. Said she would likely leave what little she had to her sister's children, Garson Talmadge's kids. That she had no one else. She knew of an attorney, but she had no car and didn't know when she might get to see him. She called after I offered to have my cabbie drive her down there; I had the taxi on the daily rate so it didn't cost me extra. She got an appointment. We waited and drove her back. I had time and felt sorry for the old gal. I had nothing better to do. This whole trip was a big blowoff to tell the truth of it, and now this foolishness is wasting your time, too."

While I answered, the digging stopped. They had retrieved their slugs.

"When are you going home, Mr. Kile?"

"Tomorrow morning. But I appreciate you not letting me spend my last evening in Paris alone. You sure you guys aren't with the tourist bureau?"

They said nothing more. I heard nothing more. Not even the click of the hotel room door. I stayed as I was, in the spread eagle position on the bed for a few minutes. I had guessed correctly. They didn't want the international incident of killing a celebrity writer with a huge fan base. Well, maybe not a celebrity, and maybe not a huge fan base. Let's just say a writer with a few loyal readers.

After chugging a short bottle of cognac from the minibar, I took a long hot shower. The water felt good running against the top of my head, although it did burn as it ran over the abrasions and short wire cut on my neck. I checked it in the mirror. The skin had been broken in several places, and the hot water got it bleeding again. I wrapped it in toilet paper while I finished off the other two small bottles of cognac, and a pony bottle of French champagne. Most countries prominently feature the products of their own country; America should do that as well.

I would apparently survive my memories of France, although that would not be certain until tomorrow late morning when my flight left the earthly bounds of Paris. I hoped one day I would return to take in more of the history and art of the country. I also hoped my newfound friends would be in hell by the time I came back, or, better yet, be waiting to give me the opportunity to send them on their way.

Chapter 20

THE NEXT MORNING, before leaving Pierre's cab, I lowered the armrest in the center of the backseat. After pulling free the Velcro strap, I opened the ski storage area that extended forward from the trunk, and removed Chantal's diary and Camille's affidavit. The iffy decision I had made last night had paid off. Maybe it had even kept me alive.

My long flight gave me lots of time to read Chantal's diary, and to reexamine all that I had learned and what I thought it all meant. It also gave me time to decide that after this case, I would stick to writing about crime and punishment. Getting beaten up and shot at for real, was a lot more painful than for the characters in my books. Speaking against this solid reasoning was the fact that while there were women like Susan and Clarice in my novels, the femme fatales in books only walked in your mind, didn't really kiss you, and can't, how should I say this, show their appreciation in more than words.

More hours later than I want to know, I staggered into my Long Beach condo. I wanted to sleep a hundred years, but that would make shaving the next morning a bitch.

I wasn't sure what time it was when I finally did get home, my watch was still set on Paris time and I lacked the active brain cells to determine how much to adjust my watch. There were appliances all over the house that showed the time, but I didn't look at them. The modern home was crowded with appliances that each seemed to include a clock. The downside was that it seemed all but impossible to get all of them set on the same time, so they each varied somewhat. This left you less certain of the time than you were when you only had one clock in the house. Ain't progress grand? All I needed to know right then was that it was dark and had been for hours. I had never been able to just come home, go to bed, and go to sleep no matter how tired I felt when I walked through the door.

Since my divorce I hadn't really thought of any place I'd lived as home, but right now my condo felt like home. I kicked off my shoes and stripped down, then walked naked into the kitchen. The under-cabinet lighting let me see to crush some ice, drop it in an old-fashioned glass, and add a twist of lemon, all of which I drowned in two jiggers of Tullamore Dew. After one sip, things looked better. I headed out to the balcony to listen to the ocean. On the way I stepped on something hard and small. After howling and hopping a few times on the opposite foot, I found one of Asta's crunchy dog treats embedded in the soft underbelly of my foot. I smiled and wondered how the little pouch was doing, probably very well. I imagined the little dog cuddling into Susan's warm curves. These were the females in my life now, two murder suspects and a chihuahua. I say that without counting my daughters and my ex for they were no longer in my life, but they were still my life.

My relationship with Susan was only beginning, but I liked her and she had let me know she felt the same. I had a brief fantasy about her which took place right there in my kitchen. The fantasy ended with my picking up the toaster and a few other items which had been knocked to the floor. If the fantasy had been for real, I could have skipped tearing this month's page off my celibacy calendar. I longed to get to weekly celibacy calendars, but right now in my life it was enough of a challenge just thinking in terms of once a month.

Unlike my continuing and messy, yet somewhat friendly relationship with my ex-wife, my relationship with Susan was uncomplicated.

Except, I have slept with her stepmother. And I had never fantasized having a mother-daughter thing with both of them at the same time. That would be ... disgusting, maybe. Oh and there's the part about Susan's stepmother being my client who is under arrest for murdering Susan's father, who may not actually be Susan's father. I've also been in a fight, more like a tussle, with Susan's brother. We don't like each other, her brother and me. And then there's this: if I do my job well, it may end with Susan getting a couple million dollars less from her father's estate, or with her or her stepmother in prison.

Susan is incredibly beautiful and sensuous. In case you aren't aware, there is a difference, not to mention her being intelligent, fun, and easy to be with. Oh, yeah, one more thing; I'm over-the-top horny.

Okay. You're right. I admit it. My relationship with Susan is complicated, very complicated. Still, bottom line, horny trumps complicated every time.

Chapter 21

I STARTED THE morning back on the balcony with a container of yogurt, which carried a use-by date that had come-and-gone while I was France, two pieces of buttered toast and a big mug of hot coffee. I had given the building super a copy of my mailbox key and he already had keys to all the condos for emergencies. Whenever I traveled he would bring my mail up and put it inside my condo. It's amazing what good service you can get from people who claimed to be overworked by being a generous tipper. Before coming out I had picked up the mail he had left on my kitchen counter and tossed it on the tray along with my eats.

I usually took along my laptop so I could check a few stocks I own and the ball scores, but not this morning. First order of business was to prioritize a list of things that needed to be done, all of which seemed to be chanting: do me first. I needed to get Camille Trenet's affidavit to Brad Fisher, along with her sister Chantal's diary. I needed to pick up Asta and spend some time with Susan. My loins had already voted for doing that first, but my head said it would fit better nearer the end of the day than the start. I also wanted to learn more about why the FBI had been so interested in my trip to France.

I also wanted to chat with Fidge. Fill him in on my adventure in France. And, sometime or other, I needed to stop at a supermarket to get some fresh yogurt, fruit and to prove the urgency of going to the store, I had just used my last coffee filter.

I refilled my coffee cup and settled back to go through the mail which consisted of several bills and a quarterly royalty statement from my publisher. It was a good thing to get some income in the mail along with the bills. For some time I had been thinking about hiring an assistant, maybe just part time. Someone to deal with the mail, prepare the bills for payment, and respect the occasional request from a reader. Most mail from readers came as email, but I kept a post box for my readers who didn't do email. It's surprising how many folks don't. The duty roster for the prospective part-timer was already growing.

My last cellmate, Axel, was getting out of prison in about two years. He had been in since his mid twenties; I guessed his age now at mid-sixties. Some of the other old-timers described Axel as a tough and mean youngster who had dropped the chip off his shoulder as he aged and become a grand old man, kind to everyone. While Axel was inside, he had worked as a secretary of sorts for the warden and had become a whiz on the computer. Axel and I shared a cell my last two years. I knew he was scared stiff about getting out. For virtually all of his life, someone else had decided when Axel went to bed, got up, what he ate, picked out his clothes, chose when he exercised, well, you get the idea. He had not shopped for anything for forty years. He would have to learn how to drive all over again. Cars were so different and, at his age, that wouldn't be easy, nothing would. When all of this suddenly gangs up on the longtime con it can be overwhelming. More than once I'd thought about hiring Axel. I had even asked my attorney to talk to the parole board and see if Axel might get let out early. I'd like to help him ease back into society. Then again, I wasn't too keen on having a regular reminder of my lost years. I'd have to think on it more.

The mail the super had left inside included an envelope without a stamp or a return identity. The note inside had no name, but I knew Fidge's handwriting: *We must talk. Don't call. I'll expect you after the house goes dark; come to the kitchen door.*

Chapter 22

BRAD'S LEGAL ASSISTANT said the man could see me at ten-forty-five. He would be free from then until noon, but he had a lunch appointment. I showered, dressed, and made it to his office with no time to spare.

"How was Paris?" he asked for openers. "Did you have any more trouble from the FBI or the Paris Prefecture of Police?"

"Not exactly." The furrow in his brow deepened as I told him about the gunshot warning, and the damage done to the bedposts in my hotel bedroom, not to mention my neck and sense of well being.

"You weren't hurt?"

"No. They shot up bed bedposts, not me."

"Did your trip bear any fruit?"

I handed him Camille's affidavit and sat silently while he read it. Then he said, "The diary?" I handed it over and went back to being quiet. After a few minutes, he said, "I can't read all of this right now, but I will. Have you read it?"

I nodded. "In the plane. It's interesting and clearly supports all that we hoped it would. Susan and Charles are not Garson's children. The father was a French big shot, but it appears his identity died with Garson, the same with respect to whether he's a maker of weapons or a government official who was paid to grease the wheels for the deals."

"Can we find him?" Brad asked.

"Sure. All we need is DNA from the hundred or so men in powerful positions, including those who have left industry or government, and throw in those who have died since Garson's children were born."

"Oh. That ought to be easy," Brad said while shaking his head. "I'm betting the real father is still alive and still a big shot. He's the guy who ordered the shot across your bow and the visits in your hotel room."

"I agree. Maybe the FBI knows," I added as an afterthought.

"You know someone there who might talk to you?"

"Maybe, there's a woman agent in the L.A. field office that helped me a bit on one of my stories last year. I got to know her, strictly professionally speaking. With Garson being here, the L.A. office likely is heading up whatever inquiry the FBI is making."

"Can we be sure they are even making an inquiry?"

"FBI Agents Smith and Jones hauled me in for a chat when I got to Paris. That didn't happen without somebody's approval, not unless they're on somebody's pad."

"Tell me more about Camille Trenet. If we fly her in, will she make a good witness?"

"Camille is a lady who likes to take a drink, even if she has to knock you to the sidelines to get to it. But, yeah, keep her off the hooch for a couple of days and I think she'd do okay. She comes across as honest. Your biggest problem is she hates Garson. I had to promise to take her by his grave so she could spit on him. She wants to help Clarice even if she iced Garson. You'll need to coach her to call him Garson while she's on the stand."

"What does she call him?"

"That worthless man. She never said his name once the whole time I was with her."

Brad and I talked around the case a while longer, but nothing that had much meat on it. Then Brad left for his lunch appointment. His assistant had tracked down the names Sappho and Charaxus. Turns out Sappho was an ancient poetess on the Island of Lesbo who had first written of a woman's right to love another woman. Charaxus had been her brother. We still had no idea why Garson had chosen those names; my guess was sick humor.

When Brad left at eleven-thirty, I headed for the supermarket where I blew a c-note. After stopping home to unload, I gassed up my car and headed for the Los Angeles office of the FBI that was located on Wilshire Boulevard between Sepulveda Boulevard and Veteran Avenue. I parked in their free parking, which meant I paid for it as a taxpayer, rather than as a specific visitor.

The office was high up enough to give me a choice of vertigo from an elevator ride or a heart attack from trucking up the stairwell. Fortunately, this elevator was larger and less rickety than the one I had ridden to see Two Dicks at the Long Beach Police Department. That helped some, but not enough to keep me from holding my breath as well as the hand rail while the box shimmied up its cable. I hope you aren't getting the idea that I'm some wimp. I'm not. I have faced a mess of fearful situations, even listened to my bed posts getting shot up in Paris, but elevators do cause me to cower a bit. Still, I suck it up and handle it when there is no reasonable alternative. That should count for something, shouldn't it?

At the front desk I asked for Maria Martinez, one of the L.A. office's four special agents in charge. Maria had been kind enough to generously give me time last year when I needed to confirm a few details regarding the FBI for one of my novels. This time I had come unannounced; I only had to wait about three minutes.

"Hello Mr. Kile. It's nice to see you again."

"Thank you. But you've forgotten my name. It's Matt."

"Matt. How can I help you? Another novel in the works?"

"There's always another novel in the works, but that's not what brought me here today."

"You've got me curious."

"Your office is working a case. I'm not sure the exact content, but it involves a recently deceased American, Garson Talmadge. Mr. Talmadge is a former French citizen and reputed arms dealer. But I'm telling you things you already know. I'd like to find out your interest in Mr. Talmadge. I'd also like to know why the bureau had interest in my recent trip to Paris, France."

"Will you give me a few minutes, Matt? I'd like to see what I can find out that we can talk about." Maria left.

After ten minutes, Special Agent Maria Martinez returned together with a man I didn't know. Maria introduced him as Kenneth Washington, the assistant director in charge. The title meant he was the FBI top man in this field office, including the several satellite offices in the metropolitan area.

"Special Agent Martinez tells me you are inquiring about whether or not we are looking at the activities of Garson Talmadge," Assistant Director Washington said. I nodded. "What makes you think we have an interest in Mr. Talmadge?"

"Please. Let's not waste each other's time or insult one another's intelligence. Garson Talmadge is a former arms dealer who brokered weapons and related materials to Saddam Hussein. He is retired here, an American citizen, and now dead. All of which we both know. At your request,

I'm guessing, Agents Smith and Jones detained me in Paris to ask me about my visit there. Later, two detectives from the Paris Prefecture of Police tossed my hotel room and hurried my departure from France. And that doesn't include someone shooting at me on the streets of Paris, an event known to the Paris Prefecture only minutes after it happened. It took connections to get those things done to an American citizen traveling in Paris. You are also talking with Garson's daughter, Susan Talmadge, with respect to said weapons deals."

"And from that you are figuring what, Mr. Kile?"

"That you directed Agents Smith and Jones to get in my face. Either the two French detectives, whom I call Twiddle Dee and Twiddle Dum, or the bureau's Smith and Jones returned to my room the next night. There I was accosted, threatened, partially strangled for effect, and forced to watch my bed posts being shot full of holes to put the fear of France into me."

"Certainly, you do not believe the FBI fired a shot at you on the street, or was involved in beating you?"

"It is interesting that your question, 'you do not believe the FBI fired the shot,' is stated in the singular."

"I believe you described the event as 'a shot.'"

"Check the recording you are making of this meeting. I did not. I referred to it in a manner that did not identify one shot. Your knowing means either that one of your agents fired the shot, or that you have been briefed by someone in France who knows the particulars."

"I can assure you the FBI would not be a party to having even one shot fired at you, or any citizen, for any reason."

"Yes. Well, I'd also like to think the FBI would not stand by while an American citizen, Clarice Talmadge, Garson's widow, is tried for a murder you know she likely did not commit."

"Who do you figure took the shot at you, Mr. Kile?"

"I figure the shot and the other intimidations were done at the direction of French munitions manufacturers or government officials who were involved in Talmadge's weapons deals. I figure they felt squeezed a little by my visit, but even more so by your investigation. Now it's your turn to do some of the talking. Tell me, am I right or am I right?"

"Essentially you are correct, Mr. Kile."

"You need a bit more show and tell than just 'essentially you are correct, Mr. Kile.' Brad Fisher, the attorney for Clarice Talmadge will be filing the appropriate demands to gain access to your files. His defense will include the likelihood that the powers behind my being harassed in Paris killed Garson to shut him up. Logic says they did so because the bureau was getting close to muscling Garson into coming clean to keep his good standing as an American citizen."

"I agree with your reasoning as to why Garson might have been murdered. I must also tell you we have nothing probative on who shot Garson Talmadge. We are not prepared to stand up in court and say that Clarice Talmadge did not murder her husband."

"Then you can expect Mr. Fisher will give you a chance to testify at her trial that you know Garson ran weapons and that you have no evidence that Mrs. Talmadge did kill her husband. And, also, that you find creditable Mr. Fisher's argument that Europeans involved in the weapons trade may have killed Garson. In any event, I simply don't believe you would help convict an innocent, grieving widow in order to protect your precious file."

"Mr. Kile, there are others with interest in the matter of weapons sales to Saddam Hussein, and some of those parties are unaware we are interested. The testimony you are suggesting we give would tip those people off and possibly put an end to our ability to close in on them. In return, we would have nothing."

"In return, you will have self respect from knowing you have saved a widow from being jailed for a crime she did not commit. Certainly protecting American citizens is part of the FBI's mission statement."

"We aren't ready to proceed in that direction at the moment. Let's see how this develops over the next few weeks before the trail begins."

"So for now, we leave this poor woman sitting in jail, without her freedom, afraid for her life, because doing so is tactical?" It was a question for which no answer was offered.

I sat looking at Assistant Director Washington and Special Agent in Charge Maria Martinez. They sat looking at me. Then Washington asked, "Is there anything further we can do for you today, Mr. Kile?"

"Yes. I'd like the names of the French industrialists and government officials who you have identified as having been part of Garson Talmadge's weapons deals."

"I'm sorry. I cannot provide those names. In part because we lack clear evidence of their complicity, and in part because our European counterparts, who are working that part of this inquiry, have not shared those identities with us. They will not do this until they are more convinced than they are at this point that those citizens of their country are guilty."

"So, they are protecting their citizens while the FBI throws one of its citizens to the wolves?"

"We've explained our position at the moment on this matter."

"Obviously, we're talking about people of power and influence in France."

"Is there anything further, Mr. Kile?"

"For now, no. Oh, by the way, you are aware, aren't you, that Susan and Charles Talmadge are not Garson's children."

Assistant Director Washington smiled as he stood and extended his hand. I shook it and left. I had done most of the talking, but I doubted I had told them anything they didn't already know, and that told me quite a bit.

Chapter 23

I HAD CALLED Susan and invited her out to dinner. She countered with the suggestion that we eat in, at her place. I got there around six. She met me at the door with a short glass in which a small lemon wedge rested on crushed ice that peeked above a nice measure of Irish whiskey — the color is unmistakable. An hour later the three of us were enjoying medium-rare T-bones and salads; Asta skipped the salad and ate only steak, on the floor below the table. Susan had cut Asta's steak into bite sized pieces. She hadn't cut mine.

Susan asked about my trip to France, whether it was fruitful. I talked around the rough stuff, but told her about Chantal having died. She took it harder than I expected.

After the steaks and salads, we had Irish coffee. I took a sip and asked, "How long have you known that Garson was not your father?"

I had tossed that one out unexpectedly to get her honest reaction, and I got it. "For nearly four years," she said. "Charles took the news harder than me. Papa explained it to both of us."

"After all those years, why did he tell you?"

"He didn't. For some reason, I had always wondered. I don't exactly know why, but I did. In law school I took a class that included information on DNA evidence. It wasn't hard to put together what was needed for the tests."

"Did you also find out who your real father was?"

"No. Papa would not say. I pressed him, but no dice. He said he had given his word, and that he didn't want his enemies to become my enemies."

We talked all that around and around, including how his reference to "his enemies" might support a theory of someone from that world killing him. She understood that Brad Fisher would use all that in a Plan-B defense for Clarice.

Oh, in case you wondered how Susan was dressed, well, she was all woman and proud of it. As for me, I was just proud she wanted to put me into her trophy box. Although, I had to admit, her reasons for wanting to do so would not be clear until after the case. I had never taken a bribe and I wasn't about to start now, even though her bribe, if it were a bribe, would be more tempting than any I had been offered while on the force. The character of her come-on would be clear after this case wrapped. Call me a silly romantic, but I'll wait.

Before leaving I asked her about how Garson went about discussing issues with her and her brother. She admitted that her papa, not always, but regularly discussed matters with her before he made a final decision. And that he rarely did so with Charles.

"Rarely or never?"

"Well, never," she admitted. "I often encouraged him to include Charles in our discussions, but he didn't."

"So he talked most everything over with you, not Clarice or Charles, and then informed them of his decisions after they were made?"

"Yes except that he told Charles of most decisions, but rarely told Clarice. He was an old-fashioned man. Charles and I had worked for papa all our lives so he was used to our being in the loop, but Clarice was a recent entry whom he saw only as part of his personal life, not business or investment."

"One more thing. I've heard all kinds of statements about when Garson stopped dealing in weapons. What is the truth?"

"His official position is that he stopped when he decided he would come to America. Later that got revised to his stopping before he applied for U.S. citizenship. I suppose all that doesn't matter a great deal any longer. The truth is he didn't stop until the U.S. invaded Iraq; that's also when the French manufacturers stopped being willing to sell to Saddam Hussein."

"And Garson would discuss these weapons deals with you up until that point?"

"With me yes. Charles' role was more that of a courier of sorts as he would carry verbal information between Papa and France. As you can imagine, very little went into writing. Charles would pass the information to a flunky in France who would then tell the French principles. That way, Charles never needed to know the identity of the French and Middle Eastern players."

"And you?"

"Papa never gave me their names either. The things he discussed with me could effectively be discussed and decided without names. He would just say its best you not know. He would also say that the people at the other end knew I did not know their identities."

By fifteen after ten, Fidge and I were sitting at the redwood picnic table in his backyard. He had come out with his fingers through a plastic six-pack ring that held four cold beers.

The urgency of his message was about the fact that in the morning, Two-Dicks was going to the D.A. to pitch his idea of tossing me into the mix alongside Clarice even though the department didn't have anything more than some conjecture. The D.A.'s case was built on Clarice murdering Garson, but Clarice had claimed and I had confirmed she was with me, so Two-Dicks reasoned we did it together and would hang tough on our exchange of alibis. Fidge admitted that under orders from Two-Dicks he had canvassed my building. Two of my condo neighbors were ready to testify they had seen Clarice coming or going from my condo in the wee hours of the morning on several occasions.

"I had no idea the man hated me that much."

"I'm sorry, Matthew."

"Not your doing. If you hadn't done it, Dicks would have replaced you on the case. The same things would have happened, only I wouldn't know about it. Thank you for telling me, you're the best friend a man could have."

We finished our beers and opened the last two, then I said, "Is that the man's full argument? Clarice was with me during some of the time in the range of hours during which Garson was murdered, so I must have helped her murder him. And, for proof, he's got my neighbors willing to say that Clarice was in the hallway some nights coming from my place?"

"It's pretty flimsy."

"It's tissue paper, Fidge. The D.A. can't make that stand up."

"Matthew, you told me you only had a one-night stand with the woman, and that was before you knew she was married."

"That's the truth," I said. "She came down other nights, just as she did the night Garson was murdered. I know it may be hard for you to believe, but all those visits were about friendship. We were not lovers. We both know Clarice is a real looker with a permanent open-for-business sign, but, well, she was married so I didn't fool around with her."

"You see, Matthew, while that could be seen as admirable, it can always be painted to show you and she were crazy about each other and wanted the old man out of the way."

"I know that. But it's not enough to get more than suspicion of infidelity on her part. Last time I looked that's not a capital offense in California, and nobody has been arrested for infidelity since the days of the inquisitions or whenever."

We had opened the last two beers before Fidge said, "So, what're we going to do?"

"You let me handle that. Your nuts are in vise already. We gain nothing good by adding your name to Two Dicks' shit list."

"So what are you going to do?"

I told him it was best he not know. I hugged the biggest and the best friend I ever had before walking back to my car which I had parked around the corner. It was the first time we had ever hugged, and we did it knowing it was against the real-men-don't-hug creed. Then again, we didn't touch cheeks which definitely would have been over the top. The hug creed has unwritten exceptions for things like winning the World Series or other championships, or trying to keep your best pal out of prison for a second time. Lesser things, like sinking an eagle putt, only get a fist bump, which has largely replaced the high five. But either is okay because they don't involve men touching each other's bodies. But then there are exceptions to that as well, but only in sports where the guys slap each other on the rump all the time for good, but not earth-shattering achievements. I know it's confusing. I also know I've likely done nothing to help clear it up in your mind.

When I stepped around the masonry wall to approach the stairs that went up to my floor, something hit me. I went down where whoever it was hit me two more times with whatever he was hitting me with. At that point I didn't know anything other than where the blows struck. The first hit my middle back, the next two the thigh of my left leg. The weapon felt like a baseball bat, not just the hardness, but also the width and how it felt.

"Clarice is innocent and I won't stop until she'd freed." I said, figuring their reaction would tell me whether this attack was related to my investigation or a random mugging by a couple of druggies looking for money.

"Back off, Kile. This is a friendly warning. You won't get another."

The voice didn't sound like Agents Smith or Jones or Tweedle Dee and Tweedle Dum from France. The good part was when they said, "back off." That told me I'd likely walk away from this, well, limp away was more likely. But at times like this I'll settle for crawl away.

"Did I meet you guys in France last week?" They didn't answer. I didn't really think so. France had been finesse and calculated rough stuff. These two were long on muscle and short on brains. Still, I wanted to get them talking. The voice had sounded somehow familiar although forced deeper.

"Go back to your writing," one of them said. "You're no longer a cop. This is out of your league. We won't tell you again. If you make us come back, next time will end with someone shoveling dirt in your face."

They hadn't bothered to frisk me. They knew I wouldn't be packing a gun. While my inability to get a weapons permit was a matter of public record, I doubted these fellows read the public record. Instead, they worked for someone who knew. Clarice knew. So did Susan, which likely meant Charles, too. The FBI knew. And, of course, my old friend Two Dicks, who had made a personal appearance to speak against my being licensed to carry.

"Let's just kill him now," a different voice said. "Why trust that he's got the message?"

"No. This is all you're being paid to do." *So, the boss man is here.* Then the first voice said, "You've been warned, Kile. Now stay where you are." Then his voice changed like it would if he were facing a different direction. "I'll leave now. You keep him here for five more minutes, and then split."

I lay there until I heard a motorcycle start up. Then I started a move that I hoped would lead to my standing up. When I was part way off the deck the motorcycle moved closer. The sound was not right at me, but near. Then a foot pushed me back down. The rider laughed and speeded away deeper into the underground garage. I did get to my feet, sort of got to my feet and headed toward the ramp that took cars up to the street. Then I heard the motorcycle tires squeal as the bike turned around. The rider had gone for the ramp that led up to the back street. Given the hour that exit had been chained closed. I heard the bike accelerate. The rider was coming back toward me, toward the ramp to the front street, the ramp toward which I staggered. I tried to hurry, but the effort was doomed to fail. The rider would reach me before I reached the street.

When I got near the little booth in the middle, I stumbled. The bike drew closer. I anticipated another kick from the rider. I dropped to one knee and lowered my head as the motorcycle got close. Then, just as the biker swerved to get near me, I stood, leaned against the little booth and quickly raised the chain that had been lying over the pavement of the ramp. The one the building super puts up to close the entrance side while leaving the exit side open. No one drove in through the exit side after that due to the angled spikes that would puncture tires.

The chain struck the rider across his chest. The bat he was still holding skidded and bounced across the cement floor until it reached the wall where the fat end made it roll in a tight circle, then lost its energy and went still. His bike continued up the ramp without him until it charged into a tangle of evergreen bushes that had been planted where the ramp turned before reaching the street.

I staggered over to pick up the bat, staggered back to the fallen rider, and rolled him face up. When I pulled his mask off all I could think of was Mr. Clean from the TV commercials. The guy was white, head shaven, and had a small hoop earring in his right ear. I love the bikers who think they're too tough to wear helmets. He was out cold.

I went through his pockets. No identification, but he had a cell phone. I took that, also three hundred he had in his pocket, likely the fee for working me over. I was insulted I came so cheap. Still, I figured I had gone through more to earn the money than had Mr. Clean so I put the three hundred in my pocket next to the cell phone. He had no weapons other than the bat I now had. I always liked baseball. I had always liked smashing the ball over the wall. Unfortunately I didn't smash enough balls over enough walls to have a future in baseball, so I became a cop. Funny how life happens to us on the way to our dreams.

I had time to reminisce so I rolled the biker onto his back. He was still out. I considered pissing in his face to revive him. I would have except that damn DNA stuff has taken a lot of the fun out of such things. It wouldn't be cool for a pardoned con to be charged with pissing on Mr. Clean. So, I did the next best thing, I used the bat to imagine I was smashing three home runs over the wall. The first smash went into the center of his back and the other two on the rear of his left thigh. Even in my pained and woozy condition, I was certain those three blasts would have all cleared the centerfield wall at Dodger stadium.

Then I headed up to my place. It hurt to move, but the hurt told me they had not broken anything except my belief in being invincible, but that belief had been shattered while I was in prison. This sneak attack after the sneak attacks I endured in France was pretty convincing. No one came at you straight on anymore. Face to face. Mano a mano. Nowadays, it was all about guns or knives, drive-by shootings, and in this case a drive-by batting. Whatever happened to the American west? Meet at high noon in the middle of the street. The good guy wins and the bad guy goes to boot hill. The world we live in now has a lot of thugs, but we are in short supply of real tough guys.

In prison you learned to always know who was behind you or coming toward you. Your eyes slept in shifts, one, and then the other.

Right then I knew I needed to be more careful if I was going to live this kind of life and not just write about it. I also decided I would try my best from now on to stick to writing about it. But damn it was fun to do it, even if a lot of pain came along with a little fun. It was a struggle, but I got upstairs where my Irish medicine waited. I planned a liberal, internal application after which I would sleep. In the morning I would decide if I needed any further care.

Chapter 24

MY LEG HOLLERED at me from inside when I bent over to pick up the morning paper which had been left just outside my door. After coming back inside, I twisted some to pull my robe over and look at the back of my black and blue thigh in the full length mirror in the hallway. That move reminded me that Mr. Clean, playing the role of bat-man had also worked on my back. I used a handheld mirror to see the thigh-matching color on my back ran from just below my shoulders nearly to my waist.

Thank God for coffee machines that start automatically, and for my having found the time to pick up some filters yesterday afternoon. I filled the biggest mug in my kitchen, lathered a bagel, and squeezed the morning paper under my arm before heading out to the balcony where I sat with my back toward the warmth from the rising morning sun.

I went inside long enough to get the biker's cell phone. Back on the balcony I opened the phone and fumbled around until I found the window where it showed his recent calls. There were five calls from yesterday. The prior calls had all been erased. The oldest of the five numbers he had called was the same number as the last call he had made about an hour before we met in the parking garage. A different window told me he had received a call from that same number around dinner time. I called the middle three first: two bars and a motorcycle repair shop. Then I zeroed in on the number involved in the other three calls. I ran a search on the Internet and came up with some guy I'd never heard of as the owner of the phone. Thugs often use stolen phones, bought on the black market. Often these are quickly shut down after the real owner discovers they were stolen. When that happens, the thug switches to a different hot phone, and the entire process repeats itself. Still, the called number looked familiar for some reason, but I couldn't place it. When I called that number a recording on the line said this number is no longer in service, likely because it had been stolen. I thought about calling Fidge. He might find out who owned that number, but the odds weren't good and it would put Fidge in a tough spot. Two Dicks was still pushing my ex-partner to find a way to pin Garson's murder on me. If Dickson ever found out Fidge was helping me with anything, my ex-partner would be back directing traffic. For now, I'd trust my mind to eventually find why that number seemed familiar.

I opened the Long Beach Press Telegram to a banner heading across the top of the front page: KEY SECURITY, HAH! Below that was a picture of yesterday's edition of the Press Telegram propped up on Garson Talmadge's dining room table. The story rolled over to page seven where I saw two more pictures. The story confirmed part of Brad Fisher's defense: The cops had proclaimed, in part, that Clarice had to be the shooter because the deadbolt prevented anyone else from getting inside the condo. They would also claim their contention was further supported by the fact that all the keys to the Talmadge unit had been accounted for. At the end of the article was a circle around the word TRUTH with a big X which appeared to be stamped over it.

There were two more pictures on page seven and both were absolutely spectacular. The first showed a straight down photograph of the same newspaper with a door key beside it lying on a black flat cloth, ideal for a blowup to confirm it was the key to the Talmadge condo. The other picture was a wide-angle shot staged to clearly confirm it had been taken inside the Talmadge condo, the newspaper visible in the distance.

Malloy had come through big time. God bless you Tiny Tim. Ah. Now I remembered. That was Malloy's first name, Tim. Timothy Malloy, a fellow Irishman and, I imagined, a fellow lover of Irish spirits.

I called Brad who agreed things were looking good for Clarice. He wasn't certain it would get her released, but it definitely took a big bite out of the D.A.'s circumstantial case. And I expected it would also put the kibosh on Two Dicks efforts to make me out as an accomplice. Brad also told me that Blackton, Garson's business attorney, had called and asked Brad to come to his office in an hour.

"No," he answered when I asked, "Blackton didn't say why. He only said it would be good news for my client. I want you to go along, Matt. I smell something big. I could hear it in Blackton's voice. Then we'll figure out our next move."

On the way over to Blackton's office, I told Brad Fisher about my two visitors the night before. He offered to take me to his doctor or stop at the hospital. I convinced him that wasn't necessary. They can't do much for bruises and sore muscles other than apply a generous portion of bedside manner and some pain meds. It would have been different had the batting I took broken any bones, but it hadn't. At least I didn't think it had.

I needed to tell Brad about my being worked over because he might be penciled in for the next visit. There was a certain pecking order to these things. The investigator came first, then, maybe, the attorney. They could instead bump me off, but that wouldn't stop anything because Fisher could simply hire a different investigator. Whoever had hired the thugs wanted the defense of Clarice Talmadge to end, or at least be relegated to going through the motions. That meant, regardless of their threat, that they would be more likely to put the muscle on Brad than rub me out. I hoped I had that figured right.

By noon Brad Fisher and I were sitting in matching leather chairs across from Sidney Blackton, who was clearly uncomfortable.

"Sidney," Brad said for openers, "why are we here?"

Sidney Blackton reached out, his hand quivering slightly, and handed us each a copy of a one-page letter dated three days before Garson was killed. "The original I have under plastic to be turned over to the police."

I didn't yet know what the letter said, but Blackton's emotions were clearly scrambled. We read in silence:

Dear Sidney, We have an appointment in a few days to discuss the changing of my will. We didn't have a chance to talk on the phone, but I wanted you to know I have decided to increase the amount left to Clarice to half of the total and reduce what is left to the children. GR

It had taken only a moment to read, but at least a minute to find our voices after the reading. The meaning of this was immense. Why would Garson reduce the amount to his children? I mean they were not his children in a biblical sense, but he had raised them and they had remained loyal to him.

The existing will said one third to each child and the other third to Clarice. The D.A. was preparing to argue that Garson had told his son he was axing Clarice entirely. This letter said something quite different.

"Mr. Blackton," I said, "From the copies you've given us, it appears the letter had been folded as if it came in an envelope. Was it?"

"It clearly has been folded to fit a number ten business envelope. The envelope however was not with the letter."

"Is that normal? I mean throwing out the envelopes of letters?"

"Yes. The exception being when return addresses are meaningful for some reason, but that's rarely the case in my kind of practice."

Brad asked, "Sidney, when did you get this?"

"I can't say exactly. I was going through his file to see if there were any lingering matters that might still require my attention. The date on it was three days before his death. I found it this morning, while going through the file."

"You hadn't seen it before?"

"No."

"How did it get into your file?" I asked.

"I can only guess. I can't say this hasn't happened before, but not often," Blackton said. "Somehow it came in and got filed without having been seen. We have a file clerk, a law school student who comes in on a regular basis. My secretary has a tray. We both put things in it. The clerk files them away. Somehow this might have gotten into that tray and —" he left the obvious unsaid, but punctuated it with a shrug.

"Well," Blackton said, looking back and forth between Brad and myself, "this certainly punches a big hole in the argument that Clarice killed Garson because he was going to drop her from the will."

Brad looked over at me and added, "It also shows that Charles was lying about what Garson told him in the late call the night he died."

"Does it?" I countered. "A few days passed between when this letter was created and when he was killed. It is possible that Garson could have changed his mind again and called Charles and told him he would cut out Clarice, just as Charles has told the police."

"So," Blackton said, "I still have no clear idea of what Garson wanted done to his will."

"This is your area of law not mine, but wouldn't you agree," Brad asked, looking directly at Blackton, "that the only course as to the disposition of his assets is the current executed will that divides it all three ways between Clarice, Susan and Charles?"

"That's how I see it. If any of the three of them tries to argue to the contrary, we are back to conjecture since this letter says a second thing and his son will claim a third. The will is properly executed; it should prevail."

"Can we talk to your file clerk?" I asked Blackton.

"I already have. I drove over and met her between her morning classes. I took along a copy of this letter. She doesn't recall it, but that's to be expected. She files hundreds of things every week. No reason any one should stick in her mind. She pays no attention to content. But, sure, I told her you might want to speak with her." Blackton tore a sheet off a scratch pad. "This is her name and contact information. Now, may I ask you a question?"

Brad nodded. Blackton said, "Criminal law is your specialty. What are the chances of finding fingerprints on the original of this letter?"

Before Brad could answer, I jumped in. "Mr. Blackton, may I also speak with your secretary? Perhaps take her to lunch so as not to infringe on your office time, with her agreement of course."

Blackton nodded then looked to Brad, "The fingerprints?"

"Well, first off, your instinct to try to protect the original was good. As I understand it, paper is one of the hardest surfaces from which to lift prints. This is due to paper being absorbent, except for highly glossed paper, which is rarely used for writing purposes. There are techniques for chemically drawing the skin oil of the print up out of the paper, but this is not an easy process. I'm sure the police experts will give that a good effort as we'd all like to know who handled that letter. Obviously finding Garson's prints on it would be very helpful for my case."

"I should have called the police first. I'll do that as soon as you leave." Blackton nodded as if agreeing to his own decision. "I've also prepared a sworn statement as to what I have just told you." He reached out. "Here's a copy, I'll give the police the original of that as well."

"Is there anything else, Mr. Blackton," I asked.

"No. I think that's it." He stood and reached out to shake hands. Brad first, then myself. While still grasping his hand I asked. "So, Garson was doing weapons deals right up until his death, right?"

"I have no knowledge of that. I was his civil lawyer. I never asked and I never knew anything about that part of his life."

"What's your gut telling you, Sidney?" Brad asked.

"Off the record?" We both nodded. "I think he had stopped before he died. I can't give you anything hard on that. Just little stuff made me think so, nuances, like that."

"How far back?" I asked. "We know it's a guess."

"A few years, but I could be all wet about that. The only thing he ever said was that he used to do that, and he wanted me to know he had stopped when he got his U.S. citizenship and came to America."

"Thank you," Brad said, "it's off the record."

On the way down in the elevator, I'd been in too many elevators this week, I told Brad about Susan admitting that Garson had not stopped dealing until we invaded Iraq. Also about his keeping from her the names of the industrialists and government officials involved. And that they were also kept from Charles who had functioned as a liaison courier between Garson and the front men for the European connections. "My guess," I told Brad, "is if we need to ascertain about when Garson stopped doing deals, we can research Charles' schedule of flights to France." We drove out of the parking lot that serviced Sidney Blackton's office knowing that in the past few hours this case had been turned inside out and stood on its head. The D.A.'s case had become Puff the Magic Dragon. The pictures in the morning paper had destroyed any claim of the killer not being able to get a key to enter Garson's condo. And the letter we just got from Blackton heavily damaged if not destroyed the testimony of Charles Talmadge that his father planned to drop Clarice from his will. The only possible counter argument being that the letter could not be proven as being typed by Garson and it was signed with a typed GR, not even GT, his first and last initials. They might also contend that Garson had changed his mind after the letter, and before calling his son. But without any kind of support, that dog wouldn't hunt.

"What are you doing?" Brad asked as I did a u-turn and headed back into the parking lot of Blackton's building.

"We need some support for the contention that letter came from Garson. We need to find out if he had given other typed letters of instruction to Blackton. Letters Blackton knew from the legal service he provided thereafter had come from Garson."

"I should have thought to ask." Brad said in a tone that suggested he felt disappointed with himself.

"We were both stunned by the turn of events," I said. "We had an understandable case of brain fade."

Twenty minutes later we again left Blackton's office after he had shown us two other letters he had in his file, typewritten letter from Garson. Both were signed with a capitalized, typewritten GR. Both letters were about matters that Blackton then handled for Garson Talmadge. As best as I could tell one of the letters, the more recent of the two appeared to have been typed on the same typewriter as the one in question, a typewriter with a clogged inside of the circle on a lower case "b."

"The cops will check this against the typewriter in the Talmadge condo," Brad opined.

"Good," I said. "Let the cops make your case."

Before I went to sleep, I called Fidge so we could touch base on what we had been doing. He let me know that yesterday afternoon, after he met with Sidney Blackton, he had stopped at the murder scene and picked up the typewriter in Garson's bedroom. He had called ahead and the department had their outside typewriter expert waiting when Fidge got back to the station with it. The letter Blackton had turned over to Fidge had been typed on the typewriter in Garson Talmadge's bedroom.

Chapter 25

AROUND NOON THE next day, Fidge called me on his cell. He had confronted Charles Talmadge about his claim that Garson had told him he was dropping Clarice from the will.

"Chucky didn't give an inch," Fidge said. "He still insists his father called him to say he was removing his wife from the will."

"Okay. That doesn't come as a big surprise. Any news on the fingerprints on the letter?"

"They're working on it now. I'm guessing they might be done by the time I get back to the station. After it's done, I'll call you when I can."

Two hours later, Fidge called. "The letter has no useable prints, not even partials. The letter had been handled by someone who had lotion on their hands. The brand of lotion was identified and there is a big bottle of it with a pump handle sitting near the water cooler in Blackton's office."

I had been hoping for Garson's prints, but even without that the way I saw it the D.A.'s case had drowned. Blackton would testify about finding the letter and that other similar letters had come from Garson on the same style of paper. The typewriter expert would confirm the typewriter was Garson's. That would cancel out the unconfirmed testimony from Charles Talmadge about Garson meaning to drop Clarice from his will. In poker language, a letter beats a verbal claim. All the rest the D.A. had would be diluted by the newspaper pictures showing someone else had gotten into and out of the Talmadge condo despite the locked dead bolt. The condo key security claim was bogus.

The D.A. was left holding a bag with nothing in it other than the thoughts of dirty minded and cynical people who believed that beautiful young women do not marry old, wealthy men for love. Clarice fit that description, but from my having known them I felt she had made a bargain with Garson and was holding up her end.

"Am I hearing you correctly? The District Attorney's office wishes to drop all charges against Clarice Talmadge?"

"Yes, your honor, effective immediately."

"I am entering the dismissal *with prejudice.*"

"We agree, your honor."

The *with prejudice* qualifier meant that absent a successful appeal the D.A. could not again arrest Clarice for the charge of murdering her husband. The D.A. had wanted the dismissal to be *without prejudice* so he could refile the charges without going to a higher court, but then backed off after Brad Fisher threatened a wrongful arrest suit based on their evidence having been flimsy all along. He spoke eloquently of a bumbling police department and heartless district attorney's office arresting a widow to be left to grieve in the ugliest of places without compassion or understanding.

"Mrs. Talmadge," the judge looked Clarice right in the eyes. "You are free to go, with the court's apology. I'm sure you have received a proper apology from the District Attorney."

Clarice Talmadge cheered, and hugged Brad Fisher, and then she hugged me.

"It's over, Clarice," Brad said. "You're free. Go home and get back to living your life." Then Brad shook my hand. "Thanks, Matt. I couldn't have done it without you. I hope we can work together again."

"It's over for you, counselor, not for me. We still don't know who murdered Garson Talmadge."

"That's not our job."

"No, Brad. That's not your job, but an investigator doesn't stop until the case is solved or every possible lead has been run to ground, at least not this investigator. I still need to know who and why."

After another round of glad handing and back slapping, I looked over at Fidge, who winked at me and smiled. Clarice waved to my ex-partner and smiled. Fidge lowered his head while looking back at her. I liked that. Clarice wasn't holding a grudge; at least she wasn't acting like she did. Then she twined her hands around my bicep, drew up close and whispered in my ear. "Let's go back to my place and celebrate. I feel like I haven't eaten, drank or fucked in a year."

On the way out, Susan stepped out from one of the bench seats to stand in front of us. We stopped. After one of those seemingly long, unsure moments, Susan smiled and the two women hugged. Women have much more liberal rules about hugging their own sex than do men. Women will even dance together in public, which men wouldn't do even after winning the World Series.

Things were looking good. Everybody seemed happy, but the core question remained unanswered and wouldn't let me join in their reverie: Who murdered Garson Talmadge?

The freeing of Clarice would make finding Garson's killer all the more difficult. The prospect of her unjust conviction had been the wedge to pry open more of what the FBI knew, or at least what they suspected. Now they had no reason to do so until they were ready, if ever, to coordinate with the French authorities to bring more of this out in the open through arrests or the ubiquitous leaked scandal. So, what did that mean? I'd have to find the killer without any help from the FBI. It sounded easy when I said it in a simple sentence, but like so much in life, the devil would be found in the details.

But I wasn't going to find the answer tonight. Clarice Talmadge was a free woman, no longer a suspect, no longer married, and no longer wearing jailhouse orange. She was back on the market and I was ready to go shopping. Tonight I would burn my celibacy calendar.

Right then, in the hallway outside the courtroom, Susan Talmadge came close enough to invite me over without being heard by the others nearby.

"The trial is over for Clarice, but I still want to know who killed your papa."

"And I'm still a suspect. Is that what you're saying?"

"I wouldn't put it that way, but I need to stay clear headed until we get to the end of the trail. Tell me you understand."

"I understand, damn it, as long as we've got a date the first night after you get your man ... or woman."

I nodded and smiled with anticipation before saying, "You're on."

"Literally, Mr. Kile?" She smiled at what we both knew was an intentional double entendre.

"Literally, Ms. Susan." I touched her cheek just before a reporter stuck a microphone in front of my face.

"Mr. Kile. Does this mean you're giving up the writing game and are back in the crime-fighting business?"

"Whoa. Whoa. I was just doing what I could to help Clarice Talmadge, a friend, who I knew to be innocent. The real hero here is Brad Fisher, attorney at law. Go see him for this story. As for me, I'm still a writer so please come back to interview me when my next novel comes out."

"It's a date," the reporter said over her shoulder as she headed toward Brad who was already standing in front of a handheld TV camera.

I turned back, but Susan was gone and in her place stood her brother Charles. "Mr. Kile, your work is over. You're terminated. Send us your final bill."

"I was employed by your stepmother's attorney. It is up to him when I'm terminated."

"His job was to represent Clarice. He's done that. She's free and can't be tried again. I repeat you're through."

"Get out of my face, worm." I tried to step around him. He put his left hand on me with his right inside his jacket. At least he was learning, this was better technique than what he had tried in his apartment. "Oh, sure, you'll going to pull your gun here on the courthouse steps with the TV cameras running ten yards away. I can tell you from my own experience that isn't smart."

"I won't warn you again, Kile."

"You've put your hands on me twice and gotten away with it because I like your sister. Under the law, that's an assault and I have the right to defend myself. You put your hands on me again, I'll knock you teeth out, and then kick you in the balls for mumbling."

Clarice was standing with Brad Fisher being interviewed. I took the opportunity to head for my car. I wanted to get home and spend a little time with Asta since she would be back with Clarice before the night was over. I also wanted to have some Irish and try to sort out the come ons from Susan and Clarice. Being involved with both of them was okay I guess, they weren't really mother and daughter, but it still sort of felt that way. My love life had been suffering from a long bout of unemployment and now I had two job offers. And I was looking forward to putting in my application for both positions.

Chapter 26

THE NEXT MORNING I slept in after a rigorous night applying for the part time job with Clarice. I would say the job was piecework, but somehow that seems tacky. I hadn't done that kind of work in a while, but it was like riding a bicycle. Clarice had met me at the door wearing a fabulous cycling outfit which really got me in the mood to swing my leg over the seat. The euphemistic bicycle had to have been a bicycle built for two because Clarice had done a significant portion of the pedaling. We had ridden around most of the night, then having gotten all hot and sweaty we took a shower and turned our attentions to eating and drinking.

After that, I had come back home to sleep. If for no other reason than to keep some, slight as it was, distance. Clarice was no longer a suspect in the eyes of the police, but she hadn't graduated to that status in my eyes, not completely. I had done my job for the defense, and I didn't really think Clarice had killed Garson, but I had seen a way where she could have. And, if that theory held up, she had first tried to use me as an alibi and then later as her champion. I would know soon enough, or at least know more soon enough. We had a lunch date and I planned to use it to test drive my Clarice-did-do-it theory.

Not being greeted by Asta had made my place seem lonely. But I put it aside and took some coffee and the morning paper out to the balcony. The sky was clear and a gentle ocean breeze had blown away Mother Nature's fog just as fully as Clarice had blown away my fog.

The newspaper was full of pictures and stories about Clarice and the dramatic surprise end to her trial which had never really started. The D.A., Fidge, and one of the press's favorites, the city's dapper chief of detectives, Captain Dickson, had all made their smiling statements about justice prevailing. There was also an interesting article titled, *The Real Garson Talmadge*. The reporter had to have been working on this article for awhile as it was chock full of suspicions and the famous unnamed sources to complete a sordid picture. Garson Talmadge had been a crusty gent who had made a wad of money selling the tools of death to despicable dictators who used those tools without compunction. The article ended with the question which still consumed me: who murdered Garson Talmadge? There were no city budgets, or other cases for me to be assigned. The Garson Talmadge case was mine and I would unwind it as long as I could find a thread to pull.

Then I left for my lunch date with Mary Stone, Sidney Blackton's secretary. We met at a nondescript lunch diner on the corner from her office. I got there early and took a booth in the corner. I had seen her in Blackton's office so I would recognize her even if she didn't recognize me.

Mary Stone was not what you would call an attractive woman. She was wearing an outfit that must have been picked out for her by the fellow who designed rental bowling shoes.

No one took rental bowling shoes home, and I figured the same was true with regard to Blackton's secretary. Still, she had a nice smile and a pleasant voice.

"Mr. Kile. First I must tell you that I've read all your books. I have your most recent one with me, *The Blackmail Club*, would you please autograph it for me. I told my book club I was having lunch with you."

"It would be my pleasure." After signing it below where I wrote in To Mary Stone, I said, "If you would like me to meet with your book club sometime, let me know. Some book clubs like speakers, some don't, so no problem either way." She thanked me effusively, and then I dove into why we were meeting. After going over the facts of the finding of the letter and there being no usable fingerprints on it, I moved into some new territory. That is I did after she had ordered a salad and ice tea. I held up two fingers to the waiter so he would bring me the same.

"Based on your recall, how often did Mr. Blackton have appointments with Garson Talmadge?"

"I would say about once a month, sometimes more often."

"Did Mrs. Talmadge ever come along with him?"

"Most of the time she did."

"Did she sit in on the meetings?"

"Oh, no, Mr. Talmadge did not want her involved in his business affairs. At least that's the reason Mr. Blackton told me, but no, she stayed outside. The two men always closed the door."

"So, there was no one else in the meeting except for Mr. Blackton, Garson Talmadge and of course the firm's file on Garson Talmadge."

"Not exactly, the files are kept behind my desk. When Mr. Blackton needed the file he would buzz me."

"Did that happen during most of the visits?"

"Mr. Blackton liked to make his clients feel like they were visiting with a friend. He kept the business trappings to a minimum. He even cleared off his desk. Then if he needed anything because of what the client and he discussed, he would ask me to bring it in. He did that with several of his real regular clients. I think they like it that way."

"And what did Clarice do while she waited? Read magazines? Talk with you?"

"All of that. Sometimes she would go out shopping close by, but mostly she sat and read from her e-reader, sometimes they were your books, Mr. Kile. Oh, and once, she went downstairs to get the men a latte at the gourmet coffee shop in the lobby."

After I got her to agree to call me Matt, I asked, "Only once?"

"Well, yes. After they left that day, Mr. Blackton reminded me they were clients and that I should go to get the coffee, not Mrs. Talmadge."

"And did you do that very often?"

"Every time they came in, after Mr. Blackton told me to be sure and do so."

"And who watched the office while you were gone? That must have taken what fifteen minutes or so?"

"About that long, yes. I'd put the phones on the recorder, you know, 'we're with other clients at the moment, please leave your number and a brief message,' like that. But most of the time the phone didn't ring. Mr. Blackton has a very select clientele. He doesn't get a lot of calls. I like that part of the job."

I smiled. "So, often Clarice Blackton was left in the office alone for fifteen minutes ... about?"

"Well, yes in the front office, but Mr. Blackton was in his office."

"With Garson Talmadge, with the door closed. Correct?"

"Yes. It was the way Mr. Blackton wanted it handled. There was never any problem."

When I had called this morning to confirm our luncheon, I had asked her to check on the date of the last time Garson and Clarice had come to their office for a meeting before the date Garson had been killed. It had been nine days.

We visited a bit longer, but nothing more came out of it that seemed relevant.

If Clarice had murdered Garson, and had gotten away with it, she could have salted her husband's file with the letter typed on Garson's typewriter. If she did, however, that would have risked it being found during the nine-day period before Garson was murdered. If that would have happened, Blackton would have told Garson who would have known the letter was a phony and whatever followed would not have gone well for Clarice.

In any event, I needed to get going. I had only eaten a salad with Mary Stone because I had a second lunch date which started in thirty minutes, with Clarice. Still, I walked Mary back to Blackton's office so I could take a look at the file cabinets behind her desk. We had been gone over an hour and the cabinets had been left unlocked.

The top Clarice wore to lunch might not have gotten her a spot in a *Girls Gone Wild* video, but it would have gotten her an audition. I drove us north and pulled into the Marie Calendar restaurant on Candlewood in the city of Lakewood, just across the border from Long Beach.

"Have you ever eaten in a Marie Calendar's Pie Shop?"

Clarice hadn't but she seemed game, so we went in. It was Saturday, and if he held to the habit he used to have, Two Dicks ate lunch there on Saturdays. It was a chance, but the worse that could happen was I'd have a pleasant lunch with Clarice in her audition outfit. Then I saw him in a corner booth. I led Clarice over figuring she would enjoy meeting a man with such a nickname. That is, if she hadn't already met him, which was why I had brought her there, to find out.

"Hello Captain Dickson. What a surprise to see you here. May we join you?"

He looked stunned. I was like the next-to-last person in the world he expected to see and the very last he expected to join him. That was just what I wanted. His eyes were on Clarice, which was understandable. I positioned myself to the side from where I could see both their faces at the same time.

"Ah. Sure. Please do," Two Dicks said. Clarice slid into the oblong booth. I entered the booth from the other side to retain a view that included both of them. So far, if Clarice knew him, she wasn't tipping it off. As for Two Dicks, his attention remained on her. Still, I couldn't be certain how often he had hiked in the hills he was surveying.

"What do you recommend?" I asked him.

"It's all good. Stick a pin in the menu, you can't go wrong." I ordered a meatloaf sandwich on grilled Parmesan sourdough, fries and a coke when the waitress came to our table. Clarice said, "Just coffee for me."

"I'm glad you weren't found guilty, Ms. Talmadge," Two Dicks said, "but it did leave us with an unsolved case." He smiled.

We talked about nothing in particular until our food came. Two Dicks pushed the catsup over toward me. Then he moved the real sugar to one side, and slid the small bowl that held the artificial sweetener toward Clarice.

"A few of my neighbors said the police were asking about me," I said to Two Dicks. "Is there anything you would like to ask me?"

"That was just routine," he said, with a dismissive wave. "You know how that goes, Matt. That phase of the investigation is over anyway. And, frankly, we have no idea where to look now. Brad Fisher's theory about your husband being killed by someone from his past looks likely. What do you think, Mrs. Talmadge?"

"I've thought that all along, ever since that weird call asking for Gar."

"You're probably right, but that takes the case outside my jurisdiction so I'm not sure how much more we local cops can do. I hope you understand. It's quite possible the Long Beach Police Department may never move this one into the solved column. I don't like admitting that, but maybe the Feds or the French police will turn up something. But then, I don't know if they even are looking into it. I'm sorry, Ma'am."

"I understand, Captain Dickson. Of course, I want my husband's killer found. But nothing is going to bring Tally back so I've just got to move on with my life."

"A very healthy attitude, Mrs. Talmadge, and may I say you are looking wonderful. Hopefully, our jail was not too unpleasant."

"Now that's a disgusting place. The worst place I have ever been and certainly the worse place I have ever slept."

"I am sorry. Please tell me you understand. It's a feeble defense for the unpleasantness you endured, but we were just doing our job. Unfortunately, we don't always get it right."

Clarice smiled. I had left them to talk while I ate and studied their faces.

"Well, folks, I need to be getting back to work. Saturday is supposed to be a day off, but not really, civil servant and all that." I slid out and Two Dicks exited the booth from my side. "Matt. May I call you Matt?" I nodded. "And may I add you did some nice work on this to help Brad Fisher. Our mothers are close and so we talk. He said that I had lost a topnotch investigator. Maybe I've been too harsh in judging you."

We shook hands and smiled. I doubted his sincerity, in part so I could still dislike him. You know how that goes. We all need a few people we don't like and so when we find one who fills that need, we hang onto the sentiment. It's one of the things that separate adults from children. Kids forgive so easily while adults are able to hold grudges.

I took Clarice home and went to my condo to call Timothy Malloy. Clarice was free in large part because of the excellent work of Timothy Malloy. I also asked if I could stop by and see him in the morning; there was something else I needed him to do.

Then I went down the hall to pet Asta, and take another bike ride with Clarice.

Chapter 27

I AWOKE A little earlier than usual, got dressed and drove over to Timothy Malloy's locksmith shop. I wanted Clarice followed. I wasn't sure for how long or exactly what I would learn from doing so, but something was still amiss when it came to Clarice Talmadge.

The one thing I knew, or strongly believed, was that Clarice and Chief of Detectives Richard Dickson had known each other before I introduced them at the restaurant. They had both performed the, glad-to-meet-you bit, but Two Dicks had tipped it off by knowing she used Sweet 'N Low. He not only moved the regular sugar to get to the artificial stuff, he spun the little bowl around so that the pink packets, not the yellow packets, were facing toward her. He knew that's what she used. That's why I had brought them together without their knowledge. To look for some little tell, and the sweetener had been their tell. Suspects will ad lib the big stuff, stage it for your viewing pleasure. It's the little stuff they aren't paying all that much attention to that reveals the lies. Things they do without forethought.

Could the why of the joint dodge they performed for me be that Clarice killed Garson with help from Two Dicks? Or, in the alternative, for her he could have just been another bed coup. And from his end of the deal, he simply didn't want it out that the department's chief of detectives had done the pelvic polka with a suspected murderess. Then again, maybe the thinking was that Dickson could help Clarice someway. Spoil a key piece of evidence, whatever. There's something connecting them, and I had to find out what that something was.

Malloy couldn't handle the tail job himself, but he stepped up to quarterback the team. One of the men who worked in his shop was an ex-con. Timothy said the man could be relied on. I figured Tim would know and a tail job doesn't require much more than staying with the target and taking plenty of pictures. Malloy said he would set it up and act as a go between so his man would never know my identity. I would get the reports and pictures through Malloy.

Brad expected that once the dust settled around Garson's estate that Clarice, Susan, and Charles would each get a little more than five million dollars. I suggested he interface with Blackton to suggest the part about Camille Trenet getting her subsistence money would work through Susan, with their three-way split being calculated after that had been allowed for.

I couldn't let go of the case until it played out, but I was still a writer and I needed to somehow schedule enough time to get back to that work. I wanted my next mystery to be out as an e-book and in paperback in about ninety days and I still had about twenty pages to write. Then the rewrites and editing and the all-important readings from a few trusted friends who have a good ear for character dialogue and a good mind for plot. Friends who would tell me the truth about what they liked and didn't, and why.

After two days of dawn-to-dusk writing I had the twenty remaining pages finished, so I took a break and called Susan to invite her out to dinner the next night. She was scheduled to work at the gentlemen's club that night, but she said she could switch and take the lunch shift and be free for dinner. "Most of the girls prefer working evenings because the tips are bigger. Come there about seven, I'll be done and ready to go." I think she wanted to see how I'd handle myself.

I read and marked up some rewrites most of the day and got to Susan's club right at seven.

"I'm glad you don't frequent these clubs, Matt."

"Who says I don't?"

"I can tell."

We talked through dinner and then moved outside to a couple of chairs that looked out toward the Long Beach pier where we had an after-dinner drink, then another. I enjoyed her company, and followed her lead. She never brought up Charles, Clarice, Garson or his murder.

"On the way back to her place, she said, "I appreciated our not talking about the case."

"I just figured you weren't ready and if you were you'd bring it up."

"You try to hide it, but you're a sensitive man, Matthew Kile. I admire that. I know you've been spending time with Clarice and that you're okay with that because you're convinced she's not guilty. Frankly I agree with that assessment. But, still, when you are similarly convinced of my innocence, I'd like a chance to compete for your attentions. Is that too forward and plainspoken of me?"

"No ma'am; I'm flattered. But at the risk of ruining the impression you just said I made, I'd like to ask you something about the case. Okay?"

"Go ahead."

"If you didn't know it, attorney Blackton told us that Clarice came to his office whenever Garson met with the attorney, but that she stayed in the lobby. That fits because you told me Garson did not include Clarice in his business or investment discussions. So, why did Clarice go along to those meetings? I mean, she just sat in the lobby and waited. That can't be fun."

"On those days Papa and Clarice would go to a little diner on Atlantic Boulevard for hamburgers and to split a piece of peanut butter pie."

"I know the place, Russell's. It's famous for its pies. When did they start going there?"

"Almost a year ago. Clarice found it one day and suggested she go with Papa to his next meeting with Blackton, whose office is just a few blocks from the restaurant. It became a thing they did … Is there anything else, Mr. Kile?"

"I'm sorry if I ruined the mood. I really am. It just didn't make sense to come back in an hour or tomorrow morning to ask you that."

"I understand," she said, "I'm just sick about all this. I want it over. I mean I want Papa's killer found, certainly. I don't know what is in the future for us, but I'd like to get on with finding out, but we can't because this case is a wall between us and I don't like that."

"I feel the same way. Goodnight."

I watched Susan walk up to her second floor unit. When she got there she turned and we swapped smiles.

On the way back to my place, Timothy Malloy called. His man had something and Malloy would have it for me by morning. His man had said it was a real zinger.

Chapter 28

I MET MALLOY for breakfast at a small local café well known for their breakfasts. The manager gave us a private corner booth.

"I do the lock work here," Tim said. "They know me." Then he slid a big envelope my way, manila with a metal clasp at the top. The glue swatch hadn't been sealed but the wings of the clasp had been spread to hold the envelope closed. I pulled out the contents, a stack of maybe six or eight photographs. As I looked through them, Tim said, "It's one of them u-lock-it places over near Signal Hill.

The first photograph showed Clarice unlocking storage unit number seventeen. From the row of similar doors that I could see in the first picture, seventeen looked about the size of a bedroom closet in a tract house. The next picture showed Clarice relocking the padlock on the door, but coming out she had a modestly bulky package under her arm. Tim's man knew his craft. The camera he used had put a date and time stamp on each picture. Clarice had been in the unit about twenty minutes. There were several more photographs, each taken with precise timing to clearly show her face or whatever else the picture was designed to reveal. The next picture showed her coming out of building four which housed unit seventeen. The last two showed Clarice in her car stopped at the curb cut from the parking lot waiting to exit the property; glancing west through the driver's window. The second showed the license plate on the rear of her car.

"Did your man see anything that suggested what she had stored or what she took out in that envelope?"

"Not his job," Malloy said. Then he dropped a key on top of the envelope, much like one might toss a chip into a poker pot. I looked at him without saying anything. My face must have said what I was thinking, "What's this?"

"He took close-ups of the padlock; I went by early this morning. This key will open the lock."

"Is your man expecting to be paid?"

"Hey. What makes the world goes round? Of course, but he works for me and did it during his shift."

I took two hundreds from my wallet and tossed them over to Tim. "Here's a tip, pass it on. He did a fine job. Thank you, Tim. Can I pay you?"

"Don't insult me, Matt."

"Then we're square. You don't owe my anything more. Next time, if there is a next time, I pay."

"Like hell. What little I've done doesn't cover you saving me three to five years of my life. Not to mention my having to surrender the money I got in that heist. If you wasn't for you, I'd have been in jail and never been able to go legit and buy my shop."

"Likewise, if it weren't for you, the jewelry job would have never been solved and those two murderers would still have been on the street. All that sounds pretty even to me."

Tim got out of the booth. While he did, I grabbed the check. He smiled. "Okay, Matt. Thanks for breakfast."

On the way back to my place which, as you know, is down the hall from Clarice's condo, I thought about the various ways to play it. I could burgle her place while she was out; Tim had given me one of two keys he had made prior to entering the Talmadge condo while I had been in France. In the alternative, I could confront her. By the time I pulled into the underground parking garage I hadn't made up my mind about anything except, for now there would be no more bike riding with Clarice.

An hour after getting home, I hadn't decided how to play it with Clarice, but I had concluded I couldn't decide until I knew what was in storage unit seventeen. I drove back to the u-store-it facility, parked, walked into building four, unlocked unit seventeen, turned on the inside light and closed the door.

Unit seventeen was empty except for two cardboard boxes. Regular storage boxes like what would be used to store office files. There was one word written on the outside of each box: video on one box and audio on the other. I opened the one labeled video. Inside were about a dozen tapes. Like the boxes, the tapes each had a label with one word: a man's name. I thumbed through them and found one with my name. Two video tapes said Blackton. The label on the next read, Dickson, in fact there were four labeled Dickson. Five other tapes had the names of men who lived in our building. I had no video player with me but I felt certain these videos were not from birthday parties.

The box labeled audio held several dozen audio tapes but they had no names, only dates or ranges of dates.

I took both boxes with me and drove home. As I drove I wondered if Clarice might have killed Garson and used a compromising tape with Garson's attorney Blackton to get him to salt his file with a letter Clarice, not Garson, had typed. She had access to Garson's typewriter. And, I was assuming the two videos gave her big-time leverage over Sidney Blackton, a married man. That would explain Blackton's nervousness when Brad and I met with him and got the letter. I mean, sure, as Blackton admitted it, his staff had screwed up, but that alone did not explain his heightened case of nerves. I had sort of blown it off at the time as Blackton being a little embarrassed and a lot whimpy. But attorneys deal with tense and difficult situations regularly and his behavior had seemed over the top.

Could Clarice have been that diabolical? She filmed herself seducing her husband's attorney, and then killed her husband, setting up the murder scene so that it pointed at her enough to get her arrested and charged. Then used films of her trysts with the attorney to set up a scenario under which she would be released in a manner making her ineligible to be re-arrested? And, let us not forget, she also had films of her seductions of Two Dicks in case she might later need the department's chief of detectives to do whatever to further weaken the case against her.

It all fit. It was all brilliant. And it was definitely diabolical. And if it was true, I had jumped into her plan to help out by using Malloy to prove someone else could have gotten inside the Talmadge condo.

Clarice was free with the charges dropped and the case now had more unanswered questions than it did before. The biggest question being: Did I consort to knowingly help Clarice beat a murder rap?

And what about Dickson? Maybe he has already helped Clarice. Maybe he went down and offed Garson using Clarice's key while she was with me. Dickson was single, so there was no threat of a marital scandal to force him to cooperate. So, if he helped her kill Garson he had to have been insanely in love with her. For some reason I couldn't see this confirmed bachelor getting himself that involved with the married Clarice. So I reasoned that if Clarice had murdered Garson she had done it herself before or after being with me. This scenario meant she had the videos of her with Dickson as a hole card. If the case somehow went bad, maybe Blackton chickened out and wouldn't plant the letter even if the scandal would destroy his marriage. If so, she would try to leverage Dickson to somehow taint the evidence or whatever. If all that is true, Dickson had never known about the film of the two of them, or Clarice having killed Garson.

First I needed to see the videos to be sure there wasn't a rational explanation for the films. I didn't think so, not for a minute, but I had to be certain. I would deal with Clarice and then I would find out whether or not Two Dicks was part of it. Then there was the mystery of the audio tapes. Were they phone calls between Clarice and these men? Maybe they were phone calls or meeting between Garson and others who participated in his weapons deals with Saddam Hussein.

Chapter 29

"OH, MATT, YOU scared me. What are you doing in here? How did you get in?"

I had surprised, Clarice. That's what I wanted to do. "Your coffeemaker comes on automatically, so I helped myself to a cup. Did you sleep well?"

"Matt. What's wrong? You seem different. Distant."

"Tell me about the video tapes?"

"What video tapes?"

"The ones you've been taking of yourself with your lovers. This one for example," I tossed one in the middle of the table. "This one features you and me although you are clearly the star. It's from when you were in my apartment before you and Garson moved in. Apparently, the camera set up is in that big purse you often carry."

"I'm sorry, Matt. I never meant for you to know."

"I'll bet. Sit down. We're going to be here awhile. I want to hear it all."

"I don't know if I want to talk about it. Take the one with you and leave."

"No dice, darling. Filming this stuff without consent can be a crime. Some of these fellows are married, most of them. Perhaps they've all been blackmailed."

"Oh. No. I would never do that. You know me better than that."

"Sure. Like I knew you couldn't have killed Garson. Like that, you mean?"

"You don't think that, do you? That I killed Tally?"

"Sit down, drink your coffee and tell me all of it. You only get one pass at it. Get it right or your collection goes to the cops. They can't get you on murder, but setting up and maybe implementing a blackmail scheme is serious in its own right."

She sat down. "Garson taught me to do it. He set up the camera for me."

"Why?"

"He enjoyed watching. It was how he could get hard. Well, how he could sometimes."

"He liked watching you?" I asked while watching her reaction.

"Yes. He got off watching me with other men. ... Look, I'm going to need something stronger than this damn coffee." She got up and went to the refrigerator. When she came back she had a bottle of red wine and a stemmed glass. "You want some, Matt?"

I held up my cup, "This is fine. Go ahead."

"That's it. Tally liked watching and truth be told, it was a turn on knowing I was being filmed. There is no more to the story."

"What did you do with the films?"

"Like I said, Garson watched them. We both did."

"Oh, come on. Most of these guys were married. You can't tell me you didn't use those films to gain some advantage. Or maybe Garson did."

"No. He wanted them for his private viewing pleasure. Hey, this isn't so way out there, you know. People do this. It's not that uncommon."

I refilled my coffee and rearranged the way I was sitting. "Sure. Folks do it, generally however, they're filming only themselves. What you're doing isn't commonplace."

What do you think I would do with them?" She stood up after asking that, put her glass down and crossed her arms."

"Oh, you could have blackmailed Lou Johnson who lives above you, no pun intended. He's loaded and totally intimidated by his wife. He'd pay to keep her from knowing."

"That's ridiculous. Tally picked Johnson. Tally wanted to see me with a guy around his own age. He wanted me to do for Johnson what I did for him."

"Why did you keep them in storage? If Garson enjoyed watching them, why not keep them handy in his bedroom?"

"We did that at first. He watched them constantly. He became obsessed with watching them. Then he would get frustrated and so angry at himself that he would get ill."

"Angry?"

"He couldn't perform nearly as frequently as he watched the films. So, they were not accomplishing what I had agreed to do them for. I told him I would not continue doing the films if he didn't turn them over to me so I could control how often we used them."

"All right, let's get back to where we were. You've explained Johnson. What about Blackton? He's married and works real hard at being respectable and he could afford to pay."

"Why would I do that, Matt? What was in it for me? Money? I'm smart enough to know that Tally would not live all that much longer." She took a drink, sat down, then stood up again. "Holy shit, you think I killed my husband. That I faked the letter and gave it to Blackton to discover in his file to get me out from under the charge of murder." Her voice had risen as she said it. She was angry.

"You have to admit that could be the way it went down."

"And pretty smart, it would be. Only thing is, I didn't murder him."

"You also had Two Dicks in your pocket."

"Who?"

"Oh, excuse me. Chief of Detectives, Captain Dickson."

"He's single. I had no leverage over him."

"Not unless he had gone all gaga over you."

"Gaga? Gaga? Now there's a mature, intelligent word for a writer."

"Dickson ran from even the idea of knowing you. He's ambitious. If the department knew he was playing hide the weasel with a murder suspect, his career would likely have suffered some damage."

"If you were in Dickson's shoes you would have wanted your involvement with a suspect to be known? You would have done the same. I went along with him when you brought me to have lunch with him. You set me up for that didn't you?"

"Yes. And I'm not going to stop until I find out who murdered Garson."

"And you've decided I'm guilty. Is that it?"

"No. But you're back in the race."

"But the charges against me were dismissed with prejudice. Brad Fisher tells me that phrase means I can't be recharged."

"As to the law, generally speaking, that's true. However, the D.A. could charge you again if he can get an appeals court to approve it. But I'm sure the media would love the story."

"And that's your plan, Matt?"

"If you did it, and the D.A. doesn't take it to the higher court, you bet I'll give it to the media, with the proof. It's not much, but at least the world would know you as a murderer."

"And if I didn't do it?"

"Then I'll be happy and, I promise you, whoever killed Garson will be sad."

"How did you know about these tapes?"

"I had you followed."

"Why?"

"After watching you and Dickson do your little dog and pony show for my benefit. It was obvious you two knew each other well."

"Will you tell me how you knew?"

"At the restaurant he pushed the artificial sweetener to you."

"That's it? He pushed me sugar?"

"No. Not sugar, the artificial stuff. To do that he had to first move the sugar, he knew you used the artificial. He even knew which of the phony ones you preferred."

"He could have guessed."

"No. It was one of those things we do under our conscious level. Seconds later, we aren't even aware we've done it. It was enough to follow you. That led to the storage unit where I found the tapes."

"I'll be getting over five million dollars. We could enjoy a grand life together."

"That's tempting, my love. You can really pedal a bicycle, but no. I'd tire of sleeping with one eye open."

"So where do we go from here? What's next, Matt?"

I got up to refill my coffee and stretch my leg and back, still sore from stopping a baseball bat. "I need to find out if any of the men in these tapes have been blackmailed. If they have, the court, realizing you had cheated them on murder, will throw the book at you for blackmail. Now, tell me about the audio tapes. What's the story on those?"

Over the next hour she told me about how she would get Garson liquored up and talking about his weapons deals. I found this pretty easy to accept for I knew from my own experience with the woman that she had a knack for getting men to talk.

From the few tapes I listened to part of I knew she had it all: names, dates, payoffs, government officials, weapons. Whatever Tally had said, she had on those audio tapes.

"In the beginning," she said, "I just found it interesting, spooky almost. But the more I listened the more I thought I might need them someday. If Tally ever tried to toss me aside like he did Chantal, his former wife who had raised the kids, I'd use the audio tapes to threaten him back in line. I was keeping our deal and I would see to it that Tally was going to hold up his end.

"Over time," she said, "I realized how amazing his mind was. Even at his advanced age, he remembered such detail without having kept any written records. He had it all, down to the ships that were used to transport and planes used, all of it. And I decided that after he died, I'd use the tapes to get a big time book deal exposing the illegal weapons trade. That'd stop that disgusting business, for a while anyway."

"And you'd make some good money."

"What's wrong with making some dough? I'd like the audio tapes back, Matt. I don't care about the sex tapes. I want the audio tapes on Tally's deals."

"Not yet."

"When?"

"When we know who killed Garson wasn't you. And even then, I'm not sure."

"Hey, here's a deal. You're a writer. You write the exposé. It'd be a whole new thing for you. Fiction writer tells all. Sales would be greater. We could split the money."

"This one's not about money, Clarice. I just haven't decided what I'll do with audios."

"What are you going to do with the films?"

"Return them probably. Depends on whether or not Blackton or Dickson helped you rub out Garson."

"Come on, Matt. This is a sweetheart deal for both of us."

"No thanks. If you didn't kill Garson, you're entitled to your inheritance. And I'm entitled to my fees for the investigation. And if you did murder your husband, somehow I'll see you get whatever punishment is possible in light of the court's ruling."

Chapter 30

I WATCHED FROM my balcony as the sun left us for today. Only those who have done this realize just how short a time it is between when the bright round globe appears to be sitting on the horizon like a ball sitting on the ground, and when the sun completely disappears below the horizon. I've never timed it, but it can't be more than three minutes.

After that I went down and walked the hard sand near the edge of the water. I loved this time of the day, early evening actually, the sky's lingering light, but not bright, colored in pastels rather than any one color or another. Good and evil, it's all so easy when we are children. The clarity of issues seen as black or white in our youth blur into so much gray as the years pile on to confuse us.

It was time to chase away some of the gray and try to find the blacks and whites.

"Matthew Kile," I said to the same desk sergeant who had been up front when I had come to the department to see Fidge at the start of this case. "I'm here to see Captain Dickson."

"He's in his office, Mr. Kile. He said you knew the way." I nodded and turned toward the stairs.

"Hello, Matt," Dickson said from his doorway, the knob in his hand.

"Captain," I said trying to hide the confusion I felt over his treating me like an earthling. I didn't know what had brought about this change in him. My latest book had made one of the top ten lists, after my earlier books had languished among the top twenty-five. Maybe this new stature meant he'd want a picture of us to add to his wall of fame.

"Come in. Sit down." I did. "What can I do for you? Are you still poking around trying to find who murdered Garson Talmadge?"

"Did Clarice Talmadge call you yesterday or this morning?"

"No." He said it straightaway. Like an easy, honest answer, or like a man knowledgeable about how to say it that way. "Why would she?"

"Look. I'm not here to pick a fight about anything, but, well, I know about the two of you. About your affair."

"What makes you think I'm involved with this woman?"

I threw a group of video tapes of him and Clarice onto his desk, bound together by one of those industrial strength, super fat rubber bands. "These."

He picked it up and looked at me. Then it registered. "Are these what I think they are?"

His manner, well, you can't fake it. Well, you could, but you'd have to be better at it than I figured Two Dicks could be.

"You betcha," I said. "There are no copies. I had thought they meant you helped Clarice do in Garson. But it doesn't figure so I'm returning them."

"Why did she do this? I mean, yeah, we did the deed a few times, but it has been quite a few months since the last time."

"Garson liked to watch them. Let's call it medicinal. And, you weren't the only leading man in her film career." I got up.

Two Dicks got up. "Do you think she really did kill Garson?"

"I still don't, but with less conviction than I felt when she was arrested."

"Why are you giving these to me? I mean thank you, but why?"

"Think of it as a gift from a fellow single man who understands just how confusing the world of romance has become. By the way, it's a mess for the ladies, too."

I walked out and headed for the stairway. Just so you won't think I'm totally foolish, I kept one of the Dickson tapes. If it turned out he did help Clarice murder Garson, I'll turn that one over to the chief of police. But first I'll make enough copies to pass around the department, anonymously of course.

After a few blocks, Susan called. "Have you made any more progress on finding out who murdered Papa?"

"No. For now I'm just letting it marinate on my mind. Like in my writing sometimes when I'm at a point where it just isn't coming together, if I leave it alone for a few hours or days when I go back to it, the pieces tend to fall into place. How are you?"

"Not so good. I haven't heard from Charlie in two days. I've gone by his place several times. Actually, I drove through his parking lot. His car's never there. And he doesn't answer his cell phone. I'm worried. I have a key to his place. I want to go in and wait, and I don't want to be alone to do it." We agreed we'd meet there. It would be quicker.

Susan and I found Charles at home. He opened the door and stepped back, his stride unsteady. He could have been on some sort of drugs, but when we got closer it was clear he had been drinking heavily. He didn't look good and the bad involved more than just the booze.

Susan offered to scramble him some eggs and make toast, but he said no. "Let me make some coffee," she said. "You could use a cup couldn't you, Matt?"

"That would be nice." I said, feeling Susan was the best person to carry the conversation, at least for now.

"None for me, sis." Charles walked over to the end table and picked up a partially filled glass sitting next to a bottle of tequila that had less in it than the amount he had poured into his glass.

"What are you doing here, Kile? You were employed to help Papa's ex. She's free now. Thanks to you, she got away with murder. Your job is done."

"Clarice didn't kill Papa," Susan said. "Give her a break. She's really not such a bad sort. And lighten up on Matt."

"She wasn't our mother, not even close. The only mother we really ever knew, Papa left in France. She's dead now. I'm sure Kile has told you that. Papa left her behind like she had been a one-night stand, a twenty-year-long one-night stand. Once she took care of raising us so he wouldn't have to, he left her high and dry. Abandoned is more like it. He was a real prick, you know? No two ways about it, a real prick. I'm glad he's dead."

"Now, Charlie. We've talked about this before. Papa wasn't the best man ever, nobody's saying he was, but he loved us. In his own way he did. Really he did."

This talk seemed too much family business, so I eased my way out onto the balcony. I could still hear from there. I've always found it fascinating how different people sounded when you could hear them, but not see them.

"If you believe that, sis, you're a bigger fool than I think you are. He took us in and kept us only as a favor to one of his buddies. Then, being stuck with us, he used Mother Chantal to raise us and as we grew, he used us as hired help. Oh, sure, he paid us well, but that's all we were, hired help. He was scum."

"He loved you Charlie. And I love you. You and I are the only real family either of us has, that we know about."

Charles huffed before mumbling something indecipherable.

I stepped into the door, but stayed on the balcony. "Sure you got a bad turn, but don't forget that without that arrangement you and Susan would have been killed as infants."

"Papa didn't step in to save us. For all he cared Hussein could have smashed our heads against a rock and thrown us in an unmarked grave. Everyone knows there were plenty of those in Iraq. It was the Frenchman who didn't want us killed. He paid Papa to protect his own conscience. And Papa took us for money and raised us to make the Frenchman beholding to him. It was about business, not family."

"We all have some kind of baggage," I said. "Life is not about whether we have it, or what it is, but how we carry it. This stuff is all your father's shortcomings, not Susan's and not yours. It's time to get on with your life." I then faded back into the darker balcony.

"That's right, Charlie," Susan said, "Matt's right about that. I love you, Bro."

"Oh, sis, if you only knew. What if I told you that when Papa called me that night he said he was dumping us from his will, leaving all the money to his bimbo wife? What if I told you that?"

"Are you telling me that?"

Listening to them from beyond the doorway, I realized the voice from the parking garage, the one that left early had been Charles. He had set up the beating, but slipped up when he had warned me to get off the case. He had deepened his voice, but listening now without seeing him I could tell. The proof came when I inadvertently slid my hand into my jacket pocket. I felt a piece of paper and opened it from curiosity to find the cell phone statement I had taken from Charles the first time I visited him in his apartment. There it was, right in front of me. I had been carrying the answer around in my pocket. The statement showed his cell phone number. The same number I had found in the list of recent calls in the biker's cell phone. The number the biker had called twice the day I was beaten. The phone number assigned to Charles Talmadge.

At that moment, all the remaining pieces rushed into place.

"Yeah, I'm telling ya that," Charles was saying to answer Susan when I again focused on listening to the two of them. "Papa called me to say he was dropping us and leaving our money to her." Then Charles took a few steps toward me on the balcony. "Even you didn't know that part, Kile."

I spoke through the doorway. "That's not exactly the way it happened, is it Charles?"

"What do you mean by that crack?"

"I meant just what I said. Your father didn't call to get your advice about dropping Clarice from his will, and he didn't call to tell you he was dropping you and your sister. Did he?"

"I don't know what you're talking about, Kile."

"Your father never called you for advice or to talk over decisions he was considering. He went to Susan, not you. He would have called Susan to see what she thought about dropping Clarice from the will."

"He wouldn't have asked sis. He knew she would tell him that wasn't the right thing to do. I love you, sis, but you're soft. Papa wouldn't have talked to you about that."

"But he wouldn't have dropped Susan. Garson loved your sister and respected her opinions. Whenever he got around to you, it was only to tell you what decision he had made."

"So what? Papa mostly liked the way sis talked him through things. But this time he decided on his own. Like I told you, sis would have tried to talk him out of it."

"You always got left in the corner when the time came to make decisions, didn't you?"

"Are you trying to make me out as having been jealous of my sister's relationship with Papa?"

"Weren't you?"

"Maybe a little, but that was Papa's fault, not sis's."

I had the ball now and I kept running toward the end zone. "So, let's get back to when Garson called you the night he died. He called you because he had made a decision. What did he really tell you that night?"

"That he was cutting Clarice down to their prenup. Just like I've been saying."

"That's not what you just told Susan."

"I was lying. Remember, I said, what if I told you, like that."

"Okay. Let that go for now. Garson's letter found at his attorney's office contradicts what you're saying now."

"Okay, Kile, you're the smart guy, at least in your own mind. What do you think happened?"

"I think Garson called to tell you he was cutting you out. Only you! He was leaving it all to Clarice and Susan. I could see him doing that."

His face went white. Charles Talmadge just stood there. Stark still as if I had reached out and slapped him, hard. I had been playing around with the thought that Garson had decided to leave it all to the women in his life, and nothing to the son he saw as a disappointment. Now I was certain.

Charles's entire body slumped as if he were an inflatable that had sprung a leak. The truth had been spoken. It was out. And in all his drunken confusion, he somehow looked relieved.

"Oh, my God," Susan said. "It's true, isn't it, Charlie?" Her brother said nothing. Susan stepped close to her brother, and she slapped him for real. And she stayed right there. Right in his face and stared. Then she repeated her question. "It's true, isn't it, Charlie? You lied to me and lied to the cops. Your lie could have helped convict Clarice. Put her in prison."

"Yes, it's true. That son of a bitch was cutting me loose. He was a cold, heartless man to the end. As for Clarice, she wasn't entitled to his money. We were. I lied for both of us."

"So, what did you do after that?" I asked, leaning back against the balcony railing. "You stewed a while in your own juices, didn't you? Then you went over there, didn't you? You went over to confront him. You used your key and went in. Clarice was down at my place. You two argued. You both got mad. He told you something like not only was he cutting you out of his will, but that he never wanted to see you again. Your papa was throwing you out like yesterday's garbage."

It was a hard message and I had delivered it as cruelly as I could. You need to get a person real angry if you want them to spill their own beans. Then I added the final blow. "The only compassionate part being that your papa didn't call you any names." I figured Garson had, and so my saying it this way was turning the knife.

"Oh, you think not. He called me every vile thing he could think of. He told me I was soft, that I was of no use to him, that I was a failure as an enforcer. That I couldn't handle a really tough man ... Well, he thought he was really tough man and I showed him."

"Charlie? You didn't — ?" Susan couldn't even finish her question, but she didn't need too. She knew the answer. Her brother had killed the man they both called papa.

"He had it coming." Charles was talking now, looking for that validation that all guilty people one day look for. "You always loved him," he said, back facing his sister. "He treated you with respect. He listened to you. He sought your advice. Since we came to America he made few decisions without consulting you."

Charles had lived through a hard upbringing, but I had no good feelings for the guy. He had wallowed in the mistreatment, letting it rot him from the inside. Maybe I felt a little pity, but damn little.

We had picked the scab off Charles's hurt and he wasn't through letting it bleed. So I went at him some more. "But you were still there for him, helping him with his weapons deals," I said. "That should have counted."

"It should have counted, but it didn't. While I was helping, Susan kept trying to get him to stop. Telling him he had plenty of money. And eventually he did stop."

"Only after America invaded Iraq," I said.

"After that," Charles said, "Susan kept pushing Papa to keep giving me money while she pushed me to go to college and get a profession. Make your way without Papa, she'd keep saying."

"Did you?"

"I didn't need a profession. Papa would die eventually and then we'd be set, Susan and me."

"But your sister went to law school."

"That's what I wanted you to do, too, Charlie. Not necessarily law school. Whatever you wanted, but have something of your own so you could be self-reliant."

"So you graduated. Big deal. You did nothing with it so what good did it do you? Right, Kile? What good did her damn law degree do for her anyway?"

"She got a good job and started a worthwhile career."

"Oh?" Charles said in a mocking tone. "I didn't know you needed a law degree to give lap dances."

"That was part of her front. I was speaking of her career with the FBI." It was a guess somewhat based on Clarice having followed Susan until she lost track of her up near the FBI office in Los Angeles. Not far from where Susan had gone to law school. It takes years to get through law school, and only those who really want it make it through. I had checked, Susan had graduated with honors.

Susan came close and put her hand on my arm. "How did you know about the FBI, Matt?"

"It's a long story. For now, let's just say it was a guess."

I didn't want to go into it with Charles standing there, but it was all part of the best explanations of a few points. Why was the FBI so interested in Garson Talmadge? He was still doing an occasional weapons deal. Why did Charles make various trips to Europe? He was the liaison between Garson and his cohorts in Europe. How did the FBI learn I was going to France? I told Susan, she likely told Charles, but he wouldn't have contact with the FBI. The only others that knew were Brad Fisher and Clarice and it would not have been in their interest to report my going. No other peg fit that hole. Susan had to have told the FBI.

"Well, sis," Charlie said accusatorially, "so you, too, struck back at Papa."

"But you killed him," she screamed. Then after standing still for a minute with her eyes closed, she tried to explain it to her brother. "I read about the American FBI when I was a girl, and knew that's what I wanted to be. When Papa decided to bring us to America I started believing it might be possible. It's why I went to law school. I hated the weapons deals, the corruption and violence. I wanted it all stopped, not just Papa's deals; although by then Papa had cut way back. The FBI was working with the French authorities. I made the Bureau realize, given my role in those deals, what I knew was rather limited. I didn't know enough about the violent part of it and the inner workings, the higher ups. I just about had the Bureau convinced they should put you and Papa in the witness protection program. You knew much more than I about the violent side of it and Papa could identify the ones at the top of it all. After that you and Papa could both leave it all behind you, have a clean law abiding life. It would have been a good finish to Papa's life. But you ruined all that, for yourself as well as for Papa. Alone, you didn't know enough to warrant the Bureau offering you the program, but I was still trying to make it happen."

Charles seemed unaffected by what he had just heard. "I had that money coming, sis. We both did. We earned it. And we would have gotten it. Everything would have worked just fine if it hadn't been for this bastard."

Charles lunged at me with his arms out, his hands against my chest. In reaction, I spun fast to one side and brought my arm up strongly into his armpit. Unsteady from drinking, his unspent forward motion along with my leverage under his arm carried him over the balcony rail.

Susan rushed to the railing. We looked down. Charles had hit the decking just short of the pool. He lay still. From the eighth floor he would lay still. Susan held me. Her face pressed against my shirt, her tears blotting on the fabric.

Charles Talmadge hadn't been a strong man, not in any way that mattered. His papa had handed him more baggage than he was able to carry.

Garson Talmadge could be summed up as a cruel man in a disgusting business. He had no friends, no true family, and the romantics would say no heart. The only woman who ever really loved him lived in an urn on a mantel in her sister's modest Paris apartment. The sister who wanted more than anything to one day spit on the grave of that worthless man.

I decided right then I would fly Camille over here so she could do just that. She had never seen America and her spitting on Garson's grave seemed the most fitting way to say: the end.

Epilogue:

CAMILLE DID SPIT on Garson's grave, twice actually. She also made friends with Susan Talmadge, her niece, in a way. The two of them felt that bond and that was all that mattered.

Susan and Clarice continued to get along, although they never really were at odds except when Charles' skullduggery caused Susan to think Clarice had murdered her papa.

Two weeks later, the FBI reassigned Susan to their New York office where she would work in a major unit formed to combat illegal weapons deals. She took along the audio tapes Clarice had made of Garson telling the details of his long and inglorious career in that illicit trade. When Clarice learned of Susan's FBI career and why she had gone to law school, Clarice agreed to turn the audio tapes over to Susan and the FBI. Clarice would make no money in a splashy book deal. Instead, the information on those tapes would be secretly used by Susan's task force to build a case against those in French industry and government who had conspired to sell the weapons.

The assignment to New York was just what Susan needed. She welcomed the change of scenery. She was strong and a solid thinker, but in the short run a new locale would ease her emotional healing. We promised to stay in touch and she invited me to visit her there whenever I wanted. I could do a lot of book signings in the New York area. From the time we spent together the last two weeks before she left, I knew I wanted to go and that I would be treated well while visiting.

Susan was quite a woman given what she had been through. My lust for her was equaled by my admiration for her.

Clarice was an enigma. It's so hard sometimes to figure out which people are wearing the good-guy white hats and which are wearing the black, bad-guy hats. Clarice, for one, clearly wore a gray hat. I, for one, still liked her.

As for me, I went back to writing about such things rather than trying to live through them. I would continue my friendship with Clarice. Susan said, "We'll be a couple thousand miles apart so we need to be practical. I'll be seeing other men in New York, so why shouldn't you see other women here? Besides Clarice and I are not blood relatives." I decided if they saw no problem with it, why should I.

I also hoped to see a bit more of my ex-wife. The few hours I occasionally spent with my ex and our daughters were still my whipped cream and cherry.

I also went before the parole board and made a formal offer of employment for my ex-cellmate, Axel. The parole board implied that he could be out soon. I was looking forward to helping Axel adjust to life on the outside.

THE END

Note to Readers

I would love to hear from you now that you have finishing reading the story. I can be reached by email at david@davidbishopbooks.com. Please, no attachments, I won't open them. For those of you who write or who aspire to write, I encourage you to continue writing until your prose lives on the pages the way it lives in your mind. If you have found errors of fact or location, I would like to hear about them. As for any errors you might imagine in spelling or punctuation or capitalization, please let me rest in peace. There are many conventions and styles with regard to these matters, and I often have characters speak incorrectly intentionally, for that is how I envision that character would speak. I promise to personally reply to all emails that respect these requests, and, with your email address, I will send you announcements for my upcoming novels; you will find the working titles and approximate release dates for each of my future stories shown near the front of this novel.

www.davidbishopbooks.com
david@davidbishopbooks.com
facebook.com/davidbishopbooks
twitter.com/davidbishop7

An excerpt from David Bishop's next novel, *The Woman* begins on the following page. For a list of David's other novels and their release dates, please see the front of this book.

The Woman

by

David Bishop

Preface:

The woman marked for death was prettier than most, but otherwise, in many ways, an ordinary woman living an ordinary life. Linda had grown up knowing only that she did not want to become her mother: housedresses, housecleaning, and a butt too wide. That mindset had led to her present state, an ex-husband and enough one-night stands to have stopped counting. No children. That had been fine in the beginning, but the last year or so she had wondered how different life might have been with children.

Linda jogged on the beach most mornings. And dined alone most evenings, before returning to her computer to enter any day trades she wanted executed upon the next opening of the financial markets. She had positioned the desk in her oceanfront condo so she could watch the comings and goings of her neighbors, whose lives seemed more exciting than her own. She was good enough at day trading to have bought her condo with cash, and several jumbo CDs that provided a steady living income.

Day trading was flexible work and Linda appreciated the insulation from the questions of coworkers: Do you have children? What happened to your marriage? She just wanted to be left alone.

Then Linda Darby went out the door to go for a walk, and nothing for her would ever again be the same.

The Woman
Chapter 1

THE MILD BEACH town night air cooled Tag's arms. Despite being well muscled, his arms felt chilly. He considered asking his partner to hold their position while he drove back to the motel to get his windbreaker; he could be back in fifteen minutes. But he knew he couldn't chance it. The call could come at any moment, letting them know Linda Darby had settled in for the night. They were ready. The drop cloth and dental instruments were in the back of the rented van. Tag's partner would have her talking nonstop in no time. No one resisted the dentist for long.

Linda Darby did not believe in the supernatural, yet tonight felt different somehow, as if gods long forgotten were whispering just beyond human hearing. She worked her tongue against the roof of her mouth. It felt dry and tasted metallic.

Her fortieth birthday was fast approaching. Perhaps her premonition had been born of that and nothing more. Forty. Like the years before, the days came and went, the seasons repeated, and all of it moved into history. Another year spent without any real change. The only constant, the horizon at sea always looked close enough to reach out and trace with her fingers. But her life remained just as she had made it, a mire. Every day aged her, gradually but definitely. Her body had not let her know this in any meaningful way, but her mind knew. Men still noticed her. Thank God. She hoped they always would, but one day they wouldn't, at least not in the same way. And through it all, time remained the true enemy.

Her subliminal awareness had started just before dusk, but Linda had forced herself through her routines. She entered her stock trades for the morning, and then called Cynthia Leclair to confirm they were on for lunch tomorrow. Her friend had sounded distant and preoccupied on the phone. Perhaps Cynthia also sensed whatever was crawling the edges of Linda's consciousness.

Her neighbors were home, but she was too restless to spend another evening watching others. She decided to go for a walk. The pleasant evening, along with the easy breeze carrying the sounds of the tossing surf might just blow away her sense of foreboding. She hadn't jogged on the beach this morning, so all this second sense could be nothing more than her body craving some activity. If so, the four-mile-roundtrip walk into town might be just what she needed to trim the crust off her mood.

She would stop in at Millie's Sea Grog. Millie's was mostly about drinking, but the place had the town's best clam chowder, not to mention a nightly crowd of area hunks wallowing in the town's bawdiest bar talk. Millie's also meant getting hit on, but, by now, the message on the boys' boner network said: Oh, sure, Linda Darby puts out, puts out rejections. She had heard the rumors: Linda is a lesbian. Linda has a secret lover. Linda is an old-fashioned girl with a steady guy overseas.

Whatever. She could deal with those guys, and she'd enjoy the laughs.

After drawing her hair back into a ponytail, and strapping on her fanny pack, she paused at the mirror. She didn't like the plumpish look that came with the pack, and neither would the fellas in Millie's. She unhooked the pack and dropped it on the chair in her bedroom. When she glanced at the ocean through the back slider, she saw low clouds on the far horizon moving horizontally, a mist more than a fog. She'd seen this pattern many times. There were no white caps out beyond the breakers; that meant mild wind off the ocean. Her prognosis, she would be back home before the dampness reached the shore. She grabbed her purse and headed out the door.

"Linda Darby's on the move," the voice said into Tag's earphone. "She walked up Ocean and angled onto Main Street, on the inland side, looks like she's heading into town. I'll let you know if she changes direction. If you don't hear from me, you know where to take her."

Linda brushed back the strands of hair the breeze had swept across her forehead and eyes, and angled onto Main Street. In the next block, a local couple came toward Linda, rollerblading their way home as they did each night after closing their glass blowing shop in town. They coasted across Main and began laboring up the only street cut into the hilly inland side. They lived on that side street, their property cut out of the tangled wild berries that crowded in wherever man had left the local land to its own devices. About one mile up, that side road deteriorated into a gravel trail fit more for deer and four wheelers than passenger cars. After another two miles that road crested over Pot Ridge, the local spine that separated the coastal dwellers from the enterprising growers who had emigrated from California's thriving marijuana fields.

    The lady rollerblader wore a lightweight sweatshirt about the color of a blouse Linda had tried on last week. The top had a cowl neckline. She had liked the fabric, just not the price. Over the years she had tried on a lot of clothes that she liked at the moment, but had forgotten about within a week. This top she had remembered, that proved something. And it had fit her just right. What the hell, you only live once. She'd stop in the House of You. Besides, she thought, the new top might just be the ticket to shake off my funk. Therapy. She smiled, thinking that maybe her doctor would give her a prescription for the top. The young doc liked to look at her, and he had a tight body she loved to ogle. But she dated no local men, no exceptions, not even for doctors.

    Downtown Sea Crest was like a morgue after dark, shrouded by a billion living stars. Linda had never understood why this one clothing store stayed open until nine. She stepped off the curb into the intersection that began her favorite stretch of downtown. The air here tasted of donuts from the nearby shop, and you didn't get love handles just smelling them. On Sundays, she often walked down to get one glazed and one cream-filled bismark. Nothing beat donuts, hot coffee and the Sunday newspaper on her deck overlooking the ocean.

    The House of You was just past the hardware store on the other side of the alley. She quickened her pace toward the store, its light reaching out across the sidewalk.

    Then, just as the pungent odors from the alley pushed the heavenly donuts from her nostrils, Linda stopped smelling everything.

The Woman
Chapter 2

A STRONG HAND clamped over Linda's mouth and nose, a wide hand, a man's hand, a suffocating hand. His strength coiled around her shoulders pinning her right arm. He wore a short-sleeve shirt, his arm carpeted with tattoos of snakes coiled around a busty topless woman. His other hand gripping her left elbow, allowed him to steer her deeper into the alley.

Oh, God.

She staggered, twisting her head in a desperate attempt to free either her mouth or nose. She fell back against his head and shoulders. He was clean shaven. His height nearly matched hers, five-eight, but he was powerful. She needed to remember all she could so she could tell the police. But at the moment her attention was riveted not on staying alive, nothing that long term, but on her desperate hunger for one more taste of air.

This is only a robbery. Only a robbery, she kept telling herself as each erratic step pulled her deeper into the darkness between the rows of two-story brick buildings.

Linda's attacker abruptly jerked her arm, navigating her around a filthy puddle in the trough gutter that centered the alley, the action momentarily easing his grip.

She sucked a mouthful of air through his smelly, tobacco-stained fingers.

He smokes. All right, that's something else I know about him.

Just as quickly, his hand retightened and the two of them went back to stumbling as if their clothes were sewn together. An idea had come with that quick breath. Her right arm was pinned against her side, but she controlled her hand. She opened it letting her purse drop to the pavement.

There's my purse. Take it. Leave me alone.

The tattooed man ignored the purse.

Desperately she searched for another idea. Something. Anything. Nothing more came.

Take my purse. Let me go. Please. Oh, please.

Linda could no longer see the brightness from Main Street. The meager light finding its way back this far had been frayed by the century of grime coating the twists and turns of the buildings lining the alley.

Her holder suddenly jerked her to a stop. The foul-smelling trough water penetrated the canvas uppers of her walking shoes. His breath slithered down the back of her t-shirt. "I'm going to let you breath. If you scream, I'll hurt you."

Tag knew the assignment was not a straight hit. First they needed to talk with Linda to learn what she knew. If the woman resisted, the dentist would start with his gum pick and battery-operated drill. No one resisted for long, but someone would hear the screams. Tag had worked under the field leader for this mission before. The man was competent, one of the best, but Tag did not agree with his decision to use the alley for this interrogation. The woman would have been home in an hour or so. They should have waited.

Linda breathed, heaving breaths, again and again. The damp, salt-rich air raced through her body. She considered screaming. But she had been warned. Instead, her voice scratched out from her dry throat. "What do you want?"

His hand moved from her arm to the top of her shoulder, his fingertips burrowing into her collarbone like a carving fork piercing a roast turkey. She buckled some hoping to alleviate the pain, but he increased the pressure.

A second man stepped out from the shadows, his belly waging war against the lower buttons of his dress shirt. His tie loose at his neck, the collar unfastened. His head in constant motion, a turret mounted on lumpy shoulders. Her holder was clearly the brawn, could this one be the brains? Not that brutalizing a woman took great brainpower.

The near electrical punch of her adrenal gland stunned Linda. Her legs buckled. Her head felt light. She didn't recognize this as a panic attack. But labels didn't matter. Escape mattered.

I'm a jogger. If I can get free, I'll have a chance.

The second man started to move toward her. No. He had only bent his knee, putting the flat of his foot up behind himself, against the wall of the building on his side.

Suddenly, the man holding her from the back jerked upward onto his toes, exhaling a loud painful grunt. From the corner of her eye Linda saw the outline of a third man fully in the shadows.

My god, he kicked the man in the balls.

Her holder released her, his hands instinctively cupping his groin as if he were holding a fledgling fallen from a bird's nest.

Kick him again. She screamed inside her head. *No, hold him and let me kick 'im. I'll drive his pecker up behind his eyes.*

In a flash, her helper slammed a brick down onto the man's spine. Then he kneed her assailant in the face, his head slamming back against the brick wall. His tattooed arms flopped like a gate with a broken hinge. He went down. Flat. His face partially submersed in the gutter trough.

Linda staggered back until her shoulders thumped that same brick wall.

As the shock of surprise wore off, the taller one on the other side of the alley brought his foot down from the wall. He reached inside his jacket. In that same moment, the third man hurled the brick he still held, striking the taller man in the shoulder. His hand inside his coat paused. In that split second, the third man drove his fist into the other man's gluttony, followed by two quick blows to his face. The taller man collapsed, a circus tent dropping to the dust of a deserted fairground.

Her helper wore a full-head stocking mask. In the shadows, she hadn't noticed. He stepped toward her. He grasped her arm and pulled her close, then touched the bottom of her chin.

Her head came up, fear occupying her face.

His warm whisper touched her ear. "You're okay." The scent of his light cologne found her nose. "Go home," he said. "Do not call the police. They cannot be trusted."

He got her walking toward the street, out of the alley. On the way she scooped up her purse, the strap seeming to reach up for the hand it knew. Ten yards from the sidewalk, he let go of her arm, turned and, betrayed only by the fading sound of his footfalls, retreated into the swallow of the darkness.

Linda spoke into that darkness. "But —"

"No buts," his voice returned from seemingly nowhere, "go straight home."

When Linda reached the sidewalk, she began walking briskly, nearly jogging, her gaze often backward. The police station was on Main Street at the corner of Oak. Three more blocks. She could make three blocks. She had to make three blocks.

At the station she grasped the door handle, pulling it part way open, and then stopped. She stood there. Then let go.

He did save me. He must have had a reason for telling me not to go to the police.

After walking to the next corner, feeling unsafe in the town where she had always felt safe, she got into a taxi, giving the driver her home address.

The hack spoke without turning his head. "Are you all right, Miss?"

The voice was louder, less of a whisper, but it sounded much like the man who saved her in the alley. She decided to find out. "If not for you," she said, "I would have died tonight."

"If you had, in that last moment, what is the one thing you would have missed most about not having in your life?"

"The right kind of a relationship with a man, maybe even a family."

"But you have been married."

"How do you know that?"

"Not important."

After a minute or two of silence, she spoke again. "I thought my husband was the right man ... My hormones keep telling me he was ... Then, eventually, I just knew ..."

"Then what?"

"I blamed the man. All my girlfriends told me I was right to leave him. I was sure at the time."

Sudden squeals and pops from the taxi's tires fighting for footing startled Linda as the cab drove off the blacktop onto the graveled roadside. "You're home," the hack said without turning his head.

"Who are you?" Linda asked.

"I teach high school social studies; I'm on vacation."

"You expect me to believe that?"

"I also teach P.E."

"I'm not going to get an honest answer, am I?"

"You were smart not to go into the police station. The authorities cannot be trusted."

"But I have to do something?"

"Yes you do. Go inside. Take a warm shower and go to bed. You will sleep. Don't worry. I got your back."

The Woman
Chapter 3

LINDA AWOKE TO the patter of windblown rain striking the window, and the crescendo of the breaking surf a hundred yards from her deck. God she loved these raw natural sounds; they allowed her to live alone without feeling isolated. She lingered, her head nested in her pillow. After a while, the rain stopped and she could hear the calls of the gulls taking flight, soaring and swooping down to skim the surface of the sea.

As always, she had left the Venetian blinds open on a slant, the morning sun and the waves acting as a gentle alarm. She parted the blinds and peered outside. Everything had that fresh look, the sky brightening wherever the sun reached through seams in the billowy clouds. A hummingbird furiously worked the airspace above her deck, thrusting its rapier-like beak in and out of the orange blossoms of a honeysuckle flourishing in one of her patio pots.

The shards of last night's terror began worming back into her mind. She poked the power button on her bedside radio, turned the volume up to cover the bathroom noises, turned on the light over the sink and opened the faucet to let the water heat. Her morning routine, everyone had one.

She had not as yet decided what, if anything, she would tell Cynthia about last night. She didn't want to worry her older friend, but she just had to tell someone, and there was no one else close enough for such a sharing. She also needed to find out why last night, on the phone, her normally upbeat friend Cynthia had sounded so melancholy.

The local radio station she habitually played each morning told of the theft of one of Sea Crest's two taxis. Then, the announcer said the thief had abandoned the cab on a side street.

Linda went still. She had ridden in that cab. As she reasoned the events, the taxi had been stolen, at least borrowed, by the man who helped her and then drove her home. He had certainly not been a cabbie for he had not asked for a fare.

I hadn't realized that until right now. And why did I tell him all that stuff about myself. Things I've never told anyone but Cynthia. Why did I do that?

Her body went rigid, the hair dryer poised above her head, warming only the air. The radio had gone on to report that two men had been found dead, murdered the announcer said, two strangers. Police Chief Benjamin McIlhenny reported having found no identification on their bodies. They had been found in the alley behind Sea Crest Donuts. Both shot in the head.

Linda's windowless bathroom shrank, cramped. The sensation of a belt tightened around her chest made her fight for the next breath, just as she had in the alley. The dead men had to be the two who attacked her. There were two men. Found in the same alley. They had been killed that same night. They had to be. Who else could they be?

She recalled the touch of the repulsive man who'd held her close. He had rough hands. And sour breath. She shuddered. Then her mind saw the cruel face of the second man, his sagging stomach.

The radio station described these killings as the first local murders ever, according to the Sea Crest Gazette, the town's twice-a-week newspaper: Wednesday and Saturday mornings. The station went on to inform its listeners that no one knew exactly which year the Gazette had issued its first edition. Old man Jory, now retired, whose family had once run the ice house just outside of town, called in to say his pa had once said the Gazette began publishing in October 1881. The paper's first lead story had been the shootout between the Earps and the Clantons at the OK Corral in Tombstone, Arizona. Since then, the Gazette had reported many murders, but none in their own quiet hamlet; that had changed this morning. The tone of the announcement almost seemed proud. Like Sea Crest had finally made the big time, had qualified to be on the map.

Such nonsense.

Her next thought struck like a claw hammer.

My mysterious helper must have killed them ... Who else? I have to tell Chief McIlhenny. No. First I want to talk with Cynthia.

Linda left her condo at eleven-fifteen so she could arrive at O'Malley's Bistro in time to get their regular table by the front window. The establishment had a side wall of stainless steel equipment that kept things cold and a back wall behind the bar crowded with more stainless equipment that kept other stuff hot. Other than the ubiquitous well-known fast food mainstays, O'Malley's Bistro along with Millie's Sea Grog comprised everything about food and drink for those who called Sea Crest home.

From the table at the front window, Linda always saw Cynthia come out of her job across the street at SMITH & CO. At sixty-two, Cynthia was twenty-two years older than

Linda, at least one hundred pounds heavier, and had weak ankles. Linda always opened the door to O'Malley's from the inside and helped Cynthia to their usual table.

SMITH & CO. occupied a plain brick, standalone building with no windows and only a small sign: SMITH & CO., CONSULTING. No glass door. No sign welcoming visitors. In fact, the building, framed by alleys on its north and south sides, projected an image that said: not welcome. Cynthia had never invited Linda to stop at the office, and had always deflected inquiries about her place of employment.

As usual, Clark Ryerson came to Linda's table. He always waited on her, trading tables with other staff when necessary. Rumor was that Clark had come to town after being hired to provide security for the marijuana growers. Then one day Clark rode his Harley into town with a horrible cut on his side, blood steadily dripping from the bottom of one pant leg of his Levi's. He told Dr. Mulvihill he'd foolishly backed into a cutting machine. The story seemed suspicious, but nothing else suggested trouble in the growers' nearly autonomous region a few miles to the east. Mulvihill stitched Clark's wound, but the man had lost a great deal of blood and needed a transfusion. Clark told the doctor to forget it; his blood was Bombay Phenotype. The state's blood banks had none. The U.S. Army had trouble getting Bombay. Only one person in every quarter-million was Bombay, and their bodies rejected blood of any other type. To Clark's surprise, the doc had one other patient with that type. Linda Darby.

The doc had called Linda at home. "You share or the odds say this fella dies." She donated what the doctor needed.

After that Clark stayed in town. He got a job waiting tables for O'Malley who ordered Clark to get rid of his earring, cut his hair above his shoulders, and work clean shaven.

Everyone had expected Clark would tell O'Malley to stick his job where the sun didn't shine, and put the coastal dwellers in the rearview mirror of his hog. Everyone was wrong. Other than drinking with some of the growers when they came to town, and letting them crash at his place when they were too drunk to drive back over Pot Ridge, Clark had apparently walked away from that part of his life. He had become a coastal dweller, a quiet citizen of Sea Crest. On more than one occasion, Linda had considered surrendering to Clark's persistence. He stood about six feet, had a well-muscled torso and a melt-you-inside smile, but he didn't fit Linda's first criteria, no locals. No relationships.

Linda drank an ice tea and a refill Clark brought, without seeing Cynthia struggling while stepping off the curb on her side of Main Street. There were never many pedestrians in Sea Crest, and those few were mostly regulars. But now and again she saw a stranger, including one passing right now, a camera case slung over his shoulder. Cynthia had recently told her about a new man in town who always carried a camera. Maybe he was that man. Cynthia, having already pitched Linda on behalf of all the eligible men she knew, had moved on to promoting men she had only observed. "After all, honey, it's the visceral stuff that rings your chimes."

The stranger had dressed to blend in. Dark shoes with soft soles, khaki pants and a windbreaker pinned down by the strap of his camera. His head covered by a dark baseball cap, nothing embroidered on its front. Linda enjoyed watching people and over the years, while waiting for Cynthia, had watched hundreds walk by SMITH & CO. Never before had anyone paid any real attention to that brick building. It had been built in the age when contractors didn't trowel off the mortar protruding between bricks. But this man had paused at the alleys on each side of the building. His pauses were nearly imperceptible, but clearly he had paused to study the unwindowed sides as if the building was a lingerie shop, and he had x-ray vision.

The man tugged his cap lower, and then suddenly faced in Linda's direction. Instinctively, she turned away. Then, realizing her reaction had been unnecessary, she looked back, taking note of a cleft in his chin, his small waist and broad shoulders.

When the man turned at the corner, Linda stared for a moment at the last space he had occupied, then went back to sipping her ice tea and watching two elderly men near the bar playing checkers, each nursing a draft beer.

When Cynthia was thirty minutes late, Linda asked Clark to bring her a Cobb salad with honey-mustard on the side, and a croissant. That is, after rejecting Clark's latest request to take her out to dinner. She said no politely, without explanation, and Clark respected her answer. While waiting for her salad, she checked her cell phone to be sure it was on and operating. It was and it held no messages. At one-thirty Linda paid the bill and left without having seen or heard from Cynthia.

The two women had been meeting at O'Malley's for lunch once a week for more than six years and never had either of them just failed to come. Linda's concern grew, but she clung to the thought that Cynthia would soon contact her with a rational explanation.

After finishing her salad, Linda walked her normal route home through the sweet smells from the donut shop. When she neared the alley into which she had been dragged, the alley in which the two dead bodies had been found, she stepped out into the street giving the mouth of the alley a wide berth. She also went cold remembering the squatty man's hard touch on her breast. She still had no idea why she had been attacked.

She had assumed a rape at the time, but that seemed likely only due to the absence of any other plausible reason. But now she knew there had to be another reason, she just had no idea what that reason could be.

The Woman is projected for an October 2011 release. Email me at david@davidbishopbooks.com to be notified when it comes out.

CPSIA information can be obtained at www.ICGtesting.com
Printed in the USA
LVOW101232041211

257713LV00001B/24/P